BOUND TO THE TUSCAN BILLIONAIRE

BY
SUSAN STEPHENS

All rights reserved including the right of reproduction in whole or in part in any form. This edition is published by arrangement with Harlequin Books S.A.

This is a work of fiction. Names, characters, places, locations and incidents are purely fictional and bear no relationship to any real life individuals, living or dead, or to any actual places, business establishments, locations, events or incidents. Any resemblance is entirely coincidental.

This book is sold subject to the condition that it shall not, by way of trade or otherwise, be lent, resold, hired out or otherwise circulated without the prior consent of the publisher in any form of binding or cover other than that in which it is published and without a similar condition including this condition being imposed on the subsequent purchaser.

® and TM are trademarks owned and used by the trademark owner and/or its licensee. Trademarks marked with ® are registered with the United Kingdom Patent Office and/or the Office for Harmonisation in the Internal Market and in other countries.

Published in Great Britain 2016
By Mills & Boon, an imprint of HarperCollins*Publishers*
1 London Bridge Street, London, SE1 9GF

© 2016 Susan Stephens

ISBN: 978-0-263-91596-9

Our policy is to use papers that are natural, renewable and recyclable products and made from wood grown in sustainable forests. The logging and manufacturing processes conform to the legal environmental regulations of the country of origin.

Printed and bound in Spain
by CPI, Barcelona

Susan Stephens was a professional singer before meeting her husband on the Mediterranean island of Malta. In true Mills & Boon Modern Romance style they met on Monday, became engaged on Friday and married three months later. Susan enjoys entertaining, travel and going to the theatre. To relax she reads, cooks and plays the piano, and when she's had enough of relaxing she throws herself off mountains on skis, or gallops through the countryside singing loudly.

Books by Susan Stephens

Mills & Boon Modern Romance

Master of the Desert
Italian Boss, Proud Miss Prim

Hot Brazilian Nights!

In the Brazilian's Debt
At the Brazilian's Command
Brazilian's Nine Months' Notice
Back in the Brazilian's Bed

The Skavanga Diamonds

Diamond in the Desert
The Flaw in His Diamond
The Purest of Diamonds?
His Forbidden Diamond

The Acostas!

The Untamed Argentinian
The Shameless Life of Ruiz Acosta
The Argentinian's Solace
A Taste of the Untamed
The Man from Her Wayward Past
Taming the Last Acosta

Visit the Author Profile page
at millsandboon.co.uk for more titles.

For my Tuscan teammates, Linda, Ann,
and the inimitable Sharon.

CHAPTER ONE

PLUNGING HER SPADE into the rich moist earth of Tuscany, Cass smiled as she reflected on her good luck in landing the job in Italy. She loved nothing more than being outdoors, using her body to the full. And where better than here, to an accompaniment of birdsong and the gurgle of a crystal-clear river. Her job was to help out at a grand estate over the planting season.

The staff had a day off on Wednesdays to break up the week, so she had the place to herself, making it all too easy to imagine that she was the chatelaine in charge of the glorious grounds—though perhaps not kitted out in mud-caked boots, braless in a skimpy vest she'd ripped on some barbed wire, topped off with a baseball cap that was as frayed and faded as her shorts!

The estate was miles from anywhere and the solitude was bliss, especially after the clamour of the supermarket where she worked back home, and being on her own was better than facing the owner of the estate. Marco di Fivizzano, an Italian industrialist, hadn't been near the place since she'd arrived. She was in no hurry to meet a man who, according to the press, was as bloodless and cold as the Cararra marble he mined.

She didn't need to worry about him, Cass mused as she stabbed her spade into the ground. She couldn't imagine a man like Marco di Fivizzano taking time out of his busy schedule to drive down from Rome to his country estate in the middle of the week. When she'd asked Maria and Giuseppe—housekeeper and handyman, respectively—if and when she was likely to meet her boss, they'd just looked at each other and shrugged.

Which was probably as well, Cass reflected as she returned to vigorously prepping the ground for the seedlings she was planting. She had no problem with hard work. Tugging her forelock was something else.

She'd always been a rebel, though a quiet one, all the rebellion being in her head. Dumb insolence, her headmistress had called it, when Cass, at seven, had refused to cry on the day she'd been made to stand on the school stage as all the pupils had trooped past. That had been the headmistress's idea to shame her on the day Cass's parents' had been arrested for drug offences. Young as she had been, she had determined never to be bullied again.

One thing still perplexed her. If her parents hadn't been the type of people the headmistress had wanted to encourage, why had the school been so keen to take their money?

She couldn't stand snobbery either. Her late father, better known as the infamous rock star Jackson Rich, could easily afford the school's extortionate fees, but that hadn't stopped the staff resenting him, his beautiful wife and Cass, his quiet, plain daughter.

Leave the past in the past where it belongs, and enjoy the Tuscan sunshine...

It was easy to do that, Cass reflected happily. Dappled sunlight sifting through the trees warmed her skin, and the scent of wild oregano was intoxicating. It was unseasonably warm for springtime in Italy, and how much better was this than her old job, squashed up in a stall, bashing the life out of a till at the local supermarket?

Closing her eyes, she smiled as she weighed up her choices: a nylon uniform that gave her static and stifled her; or the comfortable outfit she was wearing today?

No contest.

She loved working with plants, and had begged the store manager to allow her to work in the garden section, promising him that his plants would never droop again if she were in charge. He'd given her this weird look and said he liked his women clean and free from mud. She'd handed in her notice the same day.

Wiping the back of her arm across her face, she turned full circle with her arms outstretched as if sunlight were something she could touch. Birds were singing, bees were buzzing, and she could already see the fruits of her labours in fresh green shoots. On an impulse she reached for her phone to take a selfie to send to the godmother she adored and had lived with since her parents' death. When she'd taken this job she'd had it in mind to save money to buy a plane ticket for her godmother to visit her son in Australia. It would have been nice to be able buy it in time for his birthday, but that was a dream too far.

After emailing the shot, she received a reply from her godmother almost at once:

You look as if you're having a good time! Suggest a wash before anyone sees you. xoxo

With a happy laugh Cass reached up to brush away a bee, only to realise that the sound she could hear wasn't an insect but something much larger...something coming steadily closer, casting a pall over the flawless Tuscan day. Her heart rate doubled as a black helicopter swooped over the trees and hovered overhead. It blotted out the sun and obliterated the calm with noise and dust. Shielding her eyes, she tried to see who was inside, but as 'Fivizzano Inc.' was emblazoned on the side, she didn't have to test her imagination too far. Her best guess was that 'the Master', as Giovanni and Maria referred to *He who must be obeyed*, had arrived. He couldn't have told anyone he was coming or Giovanni and Maria would never have taken the day off.

She could handle it, Cass determined. She was hardly a stranger to awkward situations. She would simply stay out of his way.

Her heart beat wildly as the helicopter descended slowly like a sinister black bird, flattening the grass and driving the songbirds from the trees in a panic-stricken flock. She hadn't met anyone who travelled by helicopter since she'd been a little girl in her parents' exotic world. Thrusting her spade into the ground, she realised her hands were shaking.

Wiping her hands on her shorts, she stood rooted to the spot as the rotors slowed to a petulant whine. The passenger door opened and a tall, commanding figure, dressed immaculately for the city, sprang to the ground. Marco di Fivizzano was infinitely better looking than the press suggested, and for a moment she stood trapped in his stare.

What had got into her? She'd done nothing wrong.

Who the hell...? Marco's frown deepened. Then he remembered vaguely that his PA had mentioned something about temporary staff for the summer. He was in no mood for dealing with that now. Surely Giovanni and Maria would have laid out the ground rules—that no one approached him when he was here on his Tuscan estate.

Swearing softly under his breath, he remembered that today was Maria and Giuseppe's day off. He had been in such a hurry to leave the city for the country that his only thought had been how fast he could get here. Now he had some scruffy youth to deal with. He would have expected a new member of his gardening team to be an older and more experienced man, not some beardless boy. Coming closer, he stopped dead in his tracks as *she* turned to face him.

A grubby urchin? No make-up? Ragged clothes? Hair hidden beneath a faded baseball cap?

Legs like a colt...body like a ripe fruit, bra-free nipples pressing imperatively against her fine cotton top, her young face work-flushed and appealing...

His body responded violently and with approval. Beneath the mud, sweat, and rosy cheeks stood a very attractive young woman. The cap was crammed down hard on her head, with the brim pulled low to shade her eyes from the sun, as if she cared nothing for vanity—and that in itself was a novelty. Her clothes consisted of a ripped and mud-daubed singlet that clung lovingly to her full, pert breasts, while the frayed shorts emphasised the length of her slender legs. Striding up to her, he saw that she wasn't as young as he'd first thought, and neither was she intimidated by him—far from it. This girl wasn't afraid of anything, he sensed as she held his stare.

'And you are?' he prompted shortly.

In contrast to his irritable mood, she appeared to be relaxed and slightly bemused.

'Cassandra Rich. Your new gardener?'

Something about the surname chimed in his head, but he pushed that aside for now. Evaluating staff was his strength. The success of his business had been founded on that skill.

He stared deep into a frank, cornflower-blue gaze and ran a quick assessment. She was fresh, bright and intelligent. Inner strength, combined with the summing up *she* was giving *him*, was so novel and unexpected that he almost broke into a smile—something he did so rarely that his body took the cue and responded more insistently.

'I'm here for the summer,' she volunteered, glancing around.

Good. That gave him time to work with, he reasoned dryly.

Was he in lust with this woman?

Possibly. She was so unlike the sophisticated types he was used to she required further study—and a category all her own.

'Where's the rest of the gardening team?' he demanded, frowning.

'They're taking staggered holidays,' she explained with a shrug, drawing his attention to her bright blue eyes as she pushed a lock of her honey-gold hair away from them. 'That's why I'm here,' she added, 'to plug the gap.'

He had moved on from assessing her unusually forward manner to wondering about the rest of her hair, hidden beneath the ugly cap. He could so easily imagine freeing it and seeing it cascade down her back, just before he fisted a hank of it to pull her head back to kiss her throat.

'You can handle this entire estate on your own?' he demanded sceptically, bringing himself back with difficulty to the business side of this encounter.

'I'll have to, won't I?' she said. 'At least until the others return.'

'Yes, you will,' he confirmed sharply, still trying to work out whether her manner was impudent or overly straightforward. Meanwhile, she was staring at him inquisitively, as she might study an unusual exhibit in a gallery. They were polar opposites, curious about each other—the billionaire, hard and driven, and the mystery girl who gave casual a new edge.

His groin tightened when she smiled. He liked the way

her full lips curved and her ski-slope nose wrinkled attractively.

'I'm not as helpless as I look,' she assured him. 'And I promise I won't let you down.'

Her promise pleased him. 'If you were helpless you wouldn't be employed here.'

He turned away, knowing he should feel exhausted, but he was suddenly wide-awake.

He hadn't slept for the past twenty-four hours as he'd wrestled a trade agreement to the table that would benefit not just his own group of companies but his country. Word of his success had spread like wildfire in the power halls of Rome, attracting lean, predatory women with crippling shoes and sprayed-on clothes—another reason he had been pleased to leave the city. He could have called any one of them to accompany him to Tuscany. They were decorative and efficient and they knew the score, but none of them had appealed. He didn't know what he wanted, but it wasn't that.

'If there's anything I can do for you?' the girl called after him, stopping him in his tracks.

Was she referring to a cup of coffee or something more?

'No. Thank you.' He didn't want company, he reminded himself. At least not yet.

Success in business rode him. It also turned him on. He'd been cramped up in the city for too long. He was a physical man, bound by convention in a custom-made suit, who was forced to spend most of his working life in air-conditioned offices when what he longed for was his wild land in Tuscany. Tucked between majestic granite mountains, his country estate was an indulgence he chose not to share with anyone—certainly not with some member of his part-time staff.

'Anything at all?' she pressed.

Did she have any idea how provocative she was? As he had turned to face her she had opened her arms wide, putting her impressive breasts on show.

'Nothing. Thank you,' he repeated irritably. 'Get back to your gardening.'

He needed relief in the form of a woman, but this woman was too young and too inexperienced for him to waste his time on.

He ground his jaw with impatience when she started to follow him, and made a gesture to indicate that she should go back. The only conversation he was interested in was with real people like Maria and Giuseppe, and he resented her intrusion. She had changed the dynamics completely. She was an outsider, an interloper, and though she might hold appeal, was that smile as innocent as it looked?

If there was one thing he understood, it was the needs of a woman's body and the workings of her mind, but this girl was so different it frustrated him that he had yet to make a judgement about her.

Cass shivered involuntarily. What was wrong with her? After deciding the safest thing was to steer clear of Marco di Fivizzano, she was doing the absolute opposite. It was as if her feet had a mind of their own and had decided to follow him to the house. She should know better, when he came from the same shallow, glitzy world as her parents—

'Watch out!' he snapped.

'Sorry.' She jumped back with alarm, realising he'd stopped, and she'd almost cannoned into him.

'Have you nothing better to do than follow me to the house?' he demanded in a tone that spoke of deals hard won and nights without sleep.

'I've finished for the day,' she explained, 'and I just thought—'

'I might need help?' he queried. He stared down at her

from his great height as if she were an irritation he didn't yet have an answer to. 'If you're going to be here for the summer, you'd better tell me something about yourself.'

Her brain had stalled beneath the blazing stare. What could she tell him?

How much did she want to tell him?

'Come on—keep up,' he insisted, striding ahead. 'Let's start with where you come from.'

'England—the UK.' She had to jog to keep up with him. 'It's a region called the Lake District. I don't expect you—'

'I know the area. Family?'

The word 'family' was enough to spear her with ugly memories. That was what she didn't want to talk about, let alone take her thoughts back to the day a small bewildered child had stood at the side of the family swimming pool looking down at her parents floating, drowned after a drug-fuelled fight. She settled for the heavily censored version.

'I live with my godmother,' she explained.

'No parents?'

'Both dead.'

'My condolences.'

'It was a long time ago.'

Almost eighteen years, Cass realised with shock. She'd been so youing she'd hardly known how to grieve for them. She hadn't really known them. She'd had one carer after another while they'd been on the road with her father's band. Her emotions had died along with her parents, until her godmother had arrived to sweep Cass up in a hug. She'd taken Cass home to her modest cottage in the Lake District where the only drug was the scenery and her godmother's beautiful garden. Cass had lived there ever since, confident in her godmother's love and safe in a well-ordered life.

Maybe part of her had hidden in this security, she reflected now. That would account for a personality as compelling as Marco di Fivizzano giving her such a jolt. After her turbulent childhood, she had welcomed her godmother's cocoon of love, but increasingly had come to realise that something was missing from her life. Challenge. That was why she was here in Tuscany. This job was out of her comfort zone, and never more so than now.

'You are lucky to have a godmother to live with,' Marco di Fivizzano observed as he strode ahead of her.

'Yes. I am,' she agreed, chasing after him.

The warmth and strength of her godmother's love had never wavered, and when the day had come when Cass had been ready to fly the nest, she had helped her to get the job here in Tuscany.

She stood back when they arrived at the front door.

'Come into the house,' Fivizzano instructed when she hesitated.

She'd never been beyond the kitchen. She'd never entered the house through the front door. Her room was in an annex across the courtyard. The house was grand. She was not. She was covered in mud and she knew how hard Maria worked to keep the place spotless.

But the real reason for her hesitation was that she didn't want to be alone in the house with *him*.

'It's Giuseppe and Maria's day off,' she explained, still hovering outside the door.

'And?' he demanded impatiently.

'I'm sure if they had expected you—'

'I don't pay my staff to *expect*.'

She flinched when he added, 'Do you have a problem with that?'

Yes. She had a problem. She had never met a man so rude or so insensitive. Giuseppe and Maria would do *any-*

thing for him. Did he know that? And she was definitely not going inside the house. 'I'm sure Maria must have left something in the fridge for you to eat—'

His expression blackened. 'I beg your pardon?'

She had to remind herself that she loved this job, and that it would help to pay for her godmother's trip to Australia, and therefore she should say nothing and just get on with it.

'As Maria isn't here, you'll have to do,' he said, giving her a scathing appraisal. 'Clean yourself up and fix lunch.'

Her face blazed red beneath the arrogant stare. She had to remind herself that she had dealt with plenty of difficult customers at the supermarket. Sucking in a steadying breath, she told herself that for all his immense wealth Marco di Fivizzano was just another man.

Just another man?

She would have to remind herself of that several times a day, Cass guessed wryly, but she couldn't deny that if there was one thing she loved it was a challenge.

'My cooking isn't up to much,' she admitted, kicking off her boots.

'Do what you can.'

Senna pods in his omelette sprang to mind.

Stepping inside the beautiful old house, she was silenced for a moment. Overwhelmed by its beauty, she stared around in awe. This had to be the most beautiful hallway outside a palace. It was square and elegant...beautifully proportioned, with a high, vaulted ceiling. It was decorated with burnished antiques, as well as the most exquisite rugs—rugs Marco di Fivizzano was simply striding over in his outdoor shoes on his way to the foot of an impressive mahogany staircase.

'You can clean yourself up in the back kitchen,' he instructed, as if she were a latter-day Cinderella. 'An omelette shouldn't be beyond you.'

'I'll pick some fresh herbs—'

Her suggestion was wasted. He was already halfway up the stairs.

So much for that challenge she'd been looking forward to!

Her first assessment of Marco di Fivizzano had been correct. He was insufferably rude and incredibly insensitive. She didn't even register on his radar. He was hungry and he expected to be fed.

Then she remembered with a little pulse of interest that Marco di Fivizzano was always hungry, according to the scandal sheets—and she doubted they were talking about food. He was also a spectacular lover, according to the same magazines…

She definitely needed that wash down in cold water before she saw him again.

Having cleaned herself up, she went back into the garden and, selecting a clump of herbs, she slashed them with her knife.

No supressed emotions to deal with at all, Cass concluded with amusement.

As she walked back to the house she glanced at the upstairs windows. She could just imagine all that brute force naked beneath the shower. She'd always had a down-to-earth attitude when it came to men and sex, though living in the remote beauty of the Lake District with her godmother had hardly provided her with a wide pool of men to choose from. And when she had chosen, she'd got it wrong. She'd had one or two unsuccessful attempts to make a go of a relationship, but the men had disappointed her in a way she couldn't really explain. There had been nothing wrong with them. They just hadn't fired her imagination, and she had always dreamed of being swept away.

One thing was sure, nothing could have prepared her poor frustrated body for the arrival of a force of nature like Marco di Fivizzano.

Sheathing her knife, she wiped a hand across the back of her neck. Would he need a cold shower after meeting her? Somehow she doubted it. She guessed she was more of a wasp he'd like to swat than a beautiful butterfly he'd like to do other things with. Sex radiated from him. Even clothed in what had to be the most expensive tailoring known to man, there was something primal about him—something dark and hidden at his core—an animal energy that suggested he would consider any woman fair game.

But not this woman.

Because she had more sense?

It was time to stop daydreaming and get on with making his meal.

He took an ice-cold shower. His senses had received an unexpected jolt thanks to a most unlikely woman. He smiled grimly as he soaped himself down, imagining the type of chaos she would be creating in Maria's pristine kitchen round about now. He could only hope she'd washed her hands. He didn't care for soil in his food.

He shook his head and sent water droplets flying. Stepping out of the shower, he grabbed a towel. He felt refreshed—reinvigorated. Food followed by a few hours of vigorous sex would suit him perfectly, but it would take more than an untried girl to tempt his jaded palate. Pausing by the window, he stared out. His eyes narrowed with interest. Maybe he'd written her off too soon. She was sheathing a knife like a female Indiana Jones, and her capable, no-nonsense manner fired his senses.

* * *

She beat the living daylight out of the eggs. She had to do something to calm herself down before Genghis Khan arrived. It didn't help that all sorts of wicked thoughts were parading through her head—some including a spatula and a pair of iron-hard buttocks.

What was wrong with her?

She cleaned off the egg spatter from the wall, only for her thoughts to wander off in a new direction—to the day when she had made her first omelette. She'd been six years old and hungry. She knew now that the eggs needed watching or they'd catch and become bitter and inedible. Her first omelette had been black but she'd eaten it. She'd been hungry enough to eat the pan as well. She'd seen enough domestic disruption to last her a lifetime, and had her godmother to thank for knowing her way around a kitchen now. Anyone as sensible and good-humoured as Cass could learn to cook, her godmother had insisted when Cass had expressed doubts.

Cass had lost confidence when her parents' lives had descended into drug-fuelled chaos, but her godmother had rebuilt her brick by brick; cooking and gardening, nurturing and caring, providing the cure. These activities that were at the root of everything good, her godmother had explained, and the rewards were not only plentiful but you could eat them as well.

That had been the start of Cass finding pleasure in watching things grow. And that was why she knew she could deal with Marco di Fivizzano. Nothing he could throw at her could compare with Cass's life before she'd lived with her godmother. There were no whirlwinds in her life now, only well-ordered certainty, and that was how it was going to stay.

Tipping out a perfectly cooked omelette, she put the plate on a tray with a bowl of freshly picked salad, timing her delivery to perfection as he walked through the door.

CHAPTER TWO

IN SPITE OF his determination to treat her like any other member of staff, the sight of Cassandra Rich leaning over the kitchen sink as she scrubbed a pan thrust his basest of needs into overdrive. The swell of her hips was so perfectly displayed, though, disappointingly, she had changed her clothes—the ripped and mud-smeared singlet having been replaced by a neatly pressed T-shirt. Though a streak of mud on the side of her neck was just begging to be licked off.

'I hope you enjoy the omelette,' she said with apparent sincerity.

He dragged his attention away from one potential feast to glance at the surprisingly appetising meal she had laid out on the table. 'It looks good,' he said approvingly, 'but, where's the bread?'

He noted the flash of fire in her eyes, more typical of the way she had behaved in the garden, but then she said meekly, 'I'll get it for you, sir.'

For some reason her unusually compliant manner annoyed him too.

'For goodness' sake, call me Marco.'

He couldn't be sure if she was mocking him or not, he realised, though his best guess was yes, and blood pounded through his veins as he accepted the challenge.

'It's only a simple meal,' she explained as he grunted his thanks and sat down.

Her attempt to take out her frustration on the eggs had failed completely, Cass concluded. On second viewing, Marco di Fivizzano was even more improbably attractive than the first time she had seen him. Glancing down to make sure her top wasn't clinging to her breasts, she found her nipples were practically saluting him. In a tailor-made suit, garnished with a crisp white shirt and grey silk tie, her boss had been staggeringly attractive, but in snug-fitting jeans—she had unavoidably scanned his outline beneath them—together with a tight-fitting black top that revealed his banded muscle in more than enough detail he was an incredible sight—

'Bread?' he reminded her sharply.

He was also the rudest man she'd ever met.

She hacked at the bread with a vicious stab. The large, country kitchen seemed to be closing around her—no wonder with his arrogant animal magnetism taking up all the space.

'Have you eaten yet, Cassandra?'

She was surprised by the question but had no intention of sitting down to eat with him.

'I'm not hungry.' She was always hungry after working in the open air. 'I'll have something later.'

'See that you do,' he said, laying down his cutlery. 'You're far too thin.'

Apart from the fact that she had never once been called thin—she loved her food, and wasn't prepared to sacrifice a tasty meal for the sake of wearing jeans a size smaller—he was completely out of order, making personal comments like that.

You love this job—remember?

Heaving a calming breath, she held her tongue.

The girl kept his attention, and though she wasn't pristine, as he expected his women in Rome to be—even after cleaning herself up she had mud on her neck and more smears on her arms—at least she wasn't a simpering fool. Neither could she be grouped with the career women with whom he sometimes had a mutually satisfactory arrangement. Cassandra was unique—and not everything on his Tuscan estate was pristine, he reminded himself. He had always thought his estate better for its quirkiness.

'You're enjoying the omelette?' she guessed as he forked up the last mouthful.

'Very much,' he admitted.

He hadn't realised how hungry he was until he'd sat down to eat—or how different this kitchen was from his sleek, steel and black granite, largely untouched kitchen in Rome.

And he wouldn't change a thing, he mused as he stared around. His critical stare returned to Cassandra. 'How did you get this job?'

'A friend of my godmother's recommended me—she's another keen gardener.'

'Who employed you?' he asked, frowning.

'You did— I mean your…' Cass was stumped. Her knowledge of office hierarchy was non-existent.

'My PA?' he offered. 'She's the only one with the authority to hire my personal staff.'

'Must have been,' Cass agreed. She didn't have a clue what she was talking about. One piercing stare from those compelling eyes and her mind had been wiped clean.

'I haven't seen your CV yet,' he pressed, holding her pinned in his stare. 'What are your qualifications for this job?'

She had none, other than her passion for the plants she nurtured and the earth she turned. 'I'm self-taught,' she admitted. Her knowledge came largely from gardening books and, of course, her favourite book, *The Secret Garden*.

'And your previous job?'

She watched Marco—as she must somehow learn to think of him—push his plate away before she spoke. 'I worked the tills in my local supermarket—when I wasn't stacking shelves.'

'Education?' he prompted, the furrows on his brow deepening.

The derision directed at her by the teachers at her very expensive school had led Cass to contribute little in class, and even less when she'd sat down to take an examination. She didn't have a clutch of brilliant exam results to crow about.

'I have no formal qualifications,' she admitted, upping the tempo on her dish-clearing technique in the hope of avoiding more uncomfortable questions.

She assumed that he hadn't made the connection between the scandal of her parents' death and her surname—not yet. And why should she tell him anything more, when he revealed nothing about himself? She could understand that having his idyll trespassed on by a stranger must be an irritation for him, but a powerful, wealthy man like Marco di Fivizzano only had to make a phone call to find out everything about her. Let him do that, if he was so interested.

Calm down, she cautioned herself.

It was all very well telling herself to calm down, but she could just imagine what a man like Marco di Fivizzano would make of her past. The media had gone to town on the story of a small child wandering about in a house full of drug paraphernalia while her parents had floated dead in the swimming pool. If he knew that, then, just like everyone else, he'd make the assumption that she was tainted, when nothing could be further from the truth. She only wished she could reach back into the past as an adult to help her parents.

She sprang to attention when he got up from the table. Having him prowl around made her feel vulnerable, but he left the kitchen without a backward glance or a word of thanks.

'Rude man.' Staring out of the window, she watched him cross the yard. But he was beautiful. That easy stride… that incredible body.

Her summer had changed irrevocably now Marco di Fivizzano had arrived and only one thing was certain: her fantasies had moved on from *The Secret Garden*.

He'd had a lousy night's sleep.

He'd had no sleep. Why try to dress it up?

Dragging on his jeans, he scowled as he prowled the room. He should have had the house to himself but now *she* was in a room across the courtyard.

Lust surged in his veins at the thought that Cassandra's window was directly opposite his. He'd surfed the internet and had found out everything about her. He'd been right to recognise the name. Cassandra was the only child of the notorious rock legend Jackson Rich and his broken doll of a wife, Alexa Monroe.

So why was she working as a gardener? What had happened to all the money? Jackson Rich had been phenomenally successful. Was it possible he'd spent it all? Cassandra didn't seem to have a penny to scratch her backside with. He could only concluded that Rich's hangers-on and numerous drug-pushers had spent it for him. He had no sympathy. He'd been forced to fight every step of the way, and had had no one to rely on but himself. Rich must have been swept up in ego and success, making him an easy target. He had probably been happy to put up with the hangers-on if it had meant scoring his next fix.

For now he would give Cassandra the benefit of the doubt. It didn't follow that she had inherited her parents' weakness. If she was a yet another gold-digger, she was destined for disappointment. He didn't have a vacancy for a mud-daubed mistress in Rome. The women in Rome knew how to dress, how to talk, and how to behave—both in bed and out of it. He doubted Cassandra would be interested in acquiring any of those skills—with the possible exception of the last of them, he reflected dryly.

It was time to remind himself that he avoided complications like the plague. His childhood had proved that women couldn't be trusted, and he'd had no reason to change his mind. Cassandra Rich might be quirky and appealing, but she was no more than that.

She'd overslept! Catapulting out of bed, Cass gazed around blankly, trying to get her bearings. The simple courtyard room was the same…the house was the same…the scent of blossom coming in through the open window was the same…even the birds carolling in the crisp morning air was reassuringly the same. But everything had changed, because of Marco.

Forget the boss! She should be up and out, and working in the garden by now.

Forget him?

She would forget him, Cass determined—until she threw off the bedclothes, leapt out of bed, and rushed across to the widow, looking for *him*. Nothing like this had ever happened to her before. Tall, dark strangers with bodies made for sin had never once flown into her life in a sinister black helicopter, demanding that she feed them.

He'd demanded and *she'd* fed him. Would she handle that situation any better today?

Could anyone handle Marco di Fivizzano?

Opening the shutters, she was just in time to see him stride across the courtyard. He looked better each time she saw him—dangerous and more ruthless, more stand-well-back-unless-you-want-your-fingers-burned, in a really serious way. Especially this morning when, like last night, he'd consigned his city look to history. The men in her fantasies were always rugged and tough, but Marco made her imaginary men seem pathetic. His well-packed jeans and heavy-duty belt added fuel to her already overheated fantasies. There wasn't a spare inch of flesh on him. In jeans and a chequered shirt with the sleeves rolled back to reveal his powerful forearms, he appeared to be made entirely of hard muscle. And she would have to be made of wood not to wonder what it would be like to be in his bed.

She didn't have time for this!

Just as well, Cass thought, ducking back behind the window as Marco stared up.

Could he feel her looking at him? Were his animal instincts switched to super-alert this morning? She would have to be more discreet if she stood a chance of keeping this job.

Once she was out of the shower and wrapped in towels, she considered her vast selection of clothes. These amounted to one summer dress, 'just in case', a couple of pairs of shorts and half a dozen tops. She'd packed two pairs of jeans and a fleece in case the evenings turned cold…

And why was she taking such trouble over the selection of clothes to garden in?

Any other day and she would have grabbed the first thing to hand—shorts and a clean top. She was working with the soil, not auditioning for the role of the next notch on Marco di Fivizzano's bedpost.

So what underwear should she choose?

She scanned the unpromising heap.

Something comfortable, obviously! Did it matter, so long as she could work all day and not feel as if she was in danger of splitting her difference?

She chose her biggest knickers and a sports bra that supported her full breasts properly.

Maria and Giuseppe were back, so she dropped in a few casual questions over breakfast. They knew about as much as she did about their boss's plans for the next few days. Giuseppe mentioned something about a visit to the Fivizzano vineyards to choose some wines for an important party in Rome, but that was the only nugget she managed to glean before she went back to work.

A few days passed and then a few days more, and she barely caught a glimpse of The Boss. She kept telling herself that this was great—no pressure—but she was always on the lookout for him. She couldn't help herself. Marco di Fivizzano was a once-in-a-lifetime attraction. She gathered from Maria that he spent a lot of time inspecting his estate. It certainly felt as if she was very much 'below stairs', while he was the master of the house, whose daily life was none of her business. There was no common ground between them, no reason for them to meet—but she could dream, Cass consoled herself ruefully as she collected up her tools to go to work.

Dreams were free, and dreams were safe—or they were until Marco emerged from the house. He only had to glance her way for her heart to go crazy. He was formally dressed and had brought up the Lamborghini.

Was he going out on a date?

And why should she care?

Because smart chinos and an ice-blue shirt pointed up his pirate tan?

Lame.

But he'd teamed them with a casual, beautifully tailored taupe coloured linen jacket, and if she could just see his face…

Nope. He had lowered his sunglasses and his expression was hidden from her.

Good. Did she want him to think she was interested?

She returned to digging the trench she had started to protect her seedlings if the rains came. And those rains would come. Straightening up, she tested the air like a hound on point.

Maria had told her that although the house and estate seemed ageless and indestructible to Cass, it was, in fact, as vulnerable to the elements as any other ancient structure. The path of the river had changed over the centuries and it now presented a danger to the house. Maria had also said that in the fierce storm of 2014 trees had been uprooted and the river had flooded its banks. It was unusually still today…ominously so. Even the birds had stopped singing. She noticed Marco was also glancing at a sky tinged with acid yellow and streaked with angry clouds. She wondered briefly if he'd remembered an umbrella, and then accepted with a grin that men like Marco di Fivizzano never got wet because divine alchemy would ensure that rainclouds blew away from him.

So it fell on poor saps like me, Cass reflected wryly as she thrust her spade vigorously into the moistly yielding earth.

She was doing it again—driving him crazy with that ripe, mud-streaked body. No other woman had ever come close to affecting him the way she did. He doubted any of them had ever held a spade. They certainly didn't possess Cassandra's nonchalance when it came to using her body to the fullest. She was a very physical woman…and complex. How could she be otherwise with her past? He'd read every newspaper article he could find detailing the horrific tragedy. He knew how badly she'd been neglected until her godmother had adopted her. The media had speculated, as he was bound to, on how her parents' debauched lifestyle might have affected a young girl. His need for caution when it came to women was heading for overdrive where his new young gardener was concerned.

But since when had he been a cautious man?

Gunning the engine of his Lamborghini, he glanced across the garden to where Cassandra was swinging her spade. Her top looked as if it had shrunk in the wash and revealed inches of taut, tanned belly. He imagined dropping kisses on that smooth, silky skin and then working his way down—or up. Either way would be a pleasure for him.

He powered out of the gates, trying to distract himself from thoughts of Cassandra by thinking about all the other women he could have—maybe should have—brought along to entertain him while he was in Tuscany. Women were always eager to share his Tuscan bed, because they knew it was his private retreat, which gave it added mystery. He could think of several cute women who made him laugh—until he tired of their endless quips. There were clever women who challenged him—and gave him earache, he remembered, and beautiful women who could capture his attention and hold it for a night, but no longer. They all wanted the same thing—that his power would rub off on them, and, after that, money and sex. He had even identified a few women who would make ideal wives, but he doubted they could dig a trench, let alone turn that horticultural activity into a pornographic work of art.

Casandra's bare limbs gleamed with effort as they would after sex, and his groin tightened at he watched her thrusting her spade into the soil. She was giving it everything she'd got, as he imagined she would in bed.

Why was Marco staring at her? Cass wondered as he sped away in a storm of dust and gravel.

Why was she staring at him?

He was probably just checking she was doing her work, she reasoned sensibly. And she wouldn't look at him ever again.

That was what you said the last time.

But she meant it this time.

Did she? Marco only had to look at her for lust to stab clean through her.

That was her imagination working overtime—hopefully—she concluded as Marco's bright red Lamborghini powered away down the road. Lots of perfectly decent women lusted after the most inappropriate men, and in most cases nothing came of it—and if it did in this case, she'd run a mile. Marco di Fivizzano was one fantasy too far, she told herself sternly as his car roared away to the accompaniment of a low roll of thunder.

CHAPTER THREE

MYSTERY SOLVED. MARCO HAD gone to have lunch with the mayor. Should she feel quite so relieved when Maria told her this? Was she *jealous*?

Crazy girl! Get back out in the garden where things made sense!

Brushing her hair out of her eyes, she rammed on her cap after offering to clear up, so Maria and Giuseppe could get straight off to the fiesta in town.

'Don't get caught in the rain.' She glanced up at the darkening sky.

She waved off her friends and then contemplated the happy state of having the whole afternoon to work uninterrupted in the garden. The happy state didn't last very long. She should have listened to her own advice, Cass concluded as a flash of lightning stabbed the ground just a few feet away from her. It wasn't safe to be outdoors, but there was plenty she could do to help Maria in the kitchen.

It had quickly turned dark, and the air was as heavy as if nature was stuck in a cupboard with a headache. As the first fat spots of rain hit her in the face she collected up her tools and beat a hasty retreat. Making a dash for the kitchen door, she launched herself through it, already soaked through. There would just be time to check the windows were closed before the storm hit full force.

She raced up stairs, by which time the storm had arrived. It was like all the fiends of hell roaring around the house, testing its defences. Slapping her hands over her ears as a thunderclap shocked her out of her skin, she shrieked with alarm as lightning flashed repeatedly, and did a little dance on the spot to reassure herself that the house was still standing.

Pull yourself together! Things need to be done.

She switched on the lights and felt better immediately, but on her way downstairs they all went out again. Now the power was down. She huddled against a door in the dark, and then told herself to get over it. Finding a light switch, she flicked it on and off, more in hope than expectation. It was dead. She reached for her phone. The line was dead too. There was a house phone on the landing—

Dead.

Feeling her way carefully down the stairs, she screamed as she stepped into icy-cold water. Leaping back onto the stairs, she clung to the banister like a limpet, trying to think what to do. She told herself calmly that the house had stood for centuries, and Marco had renovated it to the nth degree, so even if the river had changed its course, the house was hardly likely to leave its foundations and float away. She was safe, and she was confident that any damage could be dealt with. If there had been similar storms in the past, Marco would have prepared for bad weather. And if the river had flooded its banks and the road from the village was closed, she was cut off, so it was up to her to sort it out.

As day turned into night in the middle of the afternoon, everyone knew that a really bad storm was coming. Making his excuses, Marco left the mayoral reception early, and as he jogged down the steps he noticed that even the stall-holders were packing up. They had all sensed the drama in the skies, and the bad weather was sweeping in much faster than expected. Some said it might be as bad as the explosive weather conditions of 2014, and with that in mind he'd called Maria and Giuseppe to warn them to stay in town. It was then they told him that Signorina Rich had never had any intention of joining them at the fiesta.

She was still at the house. And in who knew what sort of danger?

Cassandra Rich was an irritation he didn't need. Was anything straightforward where that woman was concerned? Any other woman he knew would have been drawn like a magpie to the stalls on the market, but not Cassandra. Oh, no. She had to be the one member of his staff left unaccounted for as the storm of the century approached. If the river flooded, the authorities would close the bridge and then he wouldn't get home. There were sandbags lined up outside the kitchen door, if she had the wit to use them, and an emergency generator in case the power went off.

The power would go off, he predicted, glancing again at the sky. Ribbons of lightning were slicing the boiling clouds into ugly black fragments, to a soundscape of earth-shattering thunderclaps. Then, quite suddenly, the noise subsided and it went ominously still.

Just as suddenly, rain started falling in vicious, freezing rods. Jumping into his car, he knew there wasn't a moment to lose if he was going to get across the bridge before the emergency services closed the road.

His was the last car through. Men in uniform warned him to turn back. He thanked them and then ignored them. How he longed for his rugged pick-up. He grimaced at the sound of metal crunching as he rode a bank to avoid a fallen tree. He'd almost certainly wreck the engine and the brakes. Water was rising up the wheels, and the wipers couldn't work fast enough to clear the windscreen.

He pressed on with one thought driving him. Cassandra was alone in the dark, stranded on his estate, and whether or not that was thanks to her own stubbornness, she was a member of his staff and he had a duty of care towards her. He could only imagine her relief when he arrived to save the day.

He had never been so pleased to see the house. He was less pleased to discover that floodwater was lapping around the front step. Parking up, he waded to the front door. Inserting his key, he pushed, but the door wouldn't open. He put his shoulder to it, but that made no difference. The house was in darkness. He glanced across the courtyard and called out. There was no sign of life. Where was she?

'Cassandra!'

Framing his face with his hands, he peered into one of the windows, but all he could see was blackness beyond. Turning up his collar, he retraced his steps. It brought him a moment's humour to see the ground might be flooded but Cassandra's trench was doing its job in directing the water safely away from her seedlings. He skidded to a halt at the back door. It was wide open. His heart jumped at the thought she might have run out into the night; people had died in similar weather conditions.

'Are you just going to stand there, or are you going to help me?'

He spun around at the sound of her voice. Moonlight framed her. She was at the far end of the kitchen soaked to the skin, with her hair hanging in straggles down her back as she dragged a sandbag across the floor.

'Those candles have gone out again,' she shouted as she backed into the hall. 'Can you close the door and light them for me?'

'Leave that!' He swore viciously as he tore off his jacket. He was at her side in an instant. 'You light the candles. I'll take the sandbag.'

She shook him off. The brief contact between them was electrifying.

'If you want to help me, grab another bag!' she yelled. 'The river must have burst its banks—'

'Clearly,' he said dryly, wrestling the sandbag from her grasp. He laid it down on top of the others. That was why he'd been unable to get in—and now she was rolling up his Persian carpets.

'Help me,' she insisted impatiently. 'It will be faster if the two of us do it.'

'Have you lit those candles yet?' he pressed, frowning.

'Have you got any manners?' she fired back with a scowl twice as deep as his.

He straightened up with surprise. No one had ever talked to him this way before.

'Thank you would be a start,' she told him sharply.

An almighty thunder crash brought an end to their discussion. As lightning flashed repeatedly he could see the wide-eyed shock on her face.

'You're safe,' he insisted, when nature paused to take a breath.

'If it doesn't stop raining soon, we'll be sunk—quite literally,' she said. 'Here—catch this.'

She tossed him a towel to mop up the water leaking through her barricade. Far from cowering in a corner, waiting for her white knight to arrive, Signorina Rich was firmly in control. He surprised himself by liking that.

But, then, he liked her. He couldn't help himself. He admired her grit.

'Well? Are you going to help me to roll up these rugs or not?' she demanded, glancing back at him as she lit the candles on the hall table.

There were plenty of things he would like to help Signorina Rich with, and rolling rugs wasn't at the top of his list.

It was all going well for her until she crossed the room in the half-light and caught her foot under a rug. As she stumbled he caught her close. It only took an instant to absorb how good she felt beneath his hands. Candlelight mapped the changes in her eyes from blue to black. She held her breath, almost as if she thought he was going to kiss her. Would she fight him? Would she yield hungrily? It was irrelevant to him. He might want to kiss her, he might even ache to kiss her, but he would never be so self-indulgent.

Delay was the servant of pleasure, he mused dryly as he steadied her.

'Be careful you don't trip up again.'

The look she gave him suggested that tripping up over a rug, or anything else for that matter, was the last thing on her mind.

'Shall we carry on?' she suggested. 'The rugs?' she added pointedly.

She got more brownie points for effort, and his senses got a second jolt when she brushed past him. She'd keep, he reassured his aching flesh. She wasn't going anywhere.

Having been forced to work together, Cass was surprised to discover how well they could read each other's intentions—to her surprise, they made a great team. It was certainly a pleasure watching Marco wielding his immense physical strength.

'I'll move things out of the way so you can take that rug

into the dining room,' she told him, holding her breath as Marco shouldered the weight of the wool rug as if it were a bag of feathers. Opening the door wide, she cleared a space for him, only to find him breathing down her neck. Their hands brushed. Their bodies touched. Their breath mingled as he turned around. They were just too dangerously close—

'Great job,' she said, stepping back. Now she realised that in her hurry to get away from him she had made it sound as if their positions in life had been reversed and Marco was her assistant. Oh, well. There was nothing she could do about that now. Ducking beneath his arm, she slipped away.

'Where are you going?' he demanded.

'To my bed.' She turned and shrugged. 'We've done all we can tonight. I'm going to have a bath first—try to warm up. The power may be off but the water should still be warm in the reserve tank—and I promise I won't use it all.'

'A bath in the dark?' he queried.

'I'll manage—I'll take some candles.' She glanced at his fist on the door. Was he going to try and stop her leaving? The tension between them had suddenly roared off the scale.

'You're in a hurry to get away.'

His murmur hit her straight between the shoulder blades in a deliciously dangerous quiver of awareness. 'I'm cold,' she excused herself, hugging her body and acting fragile. She doubted he was convinced, but at least he lifted his hand from the door.

'You've done well tonight,' he said as he stood back.

'And now I'm freezing,' she reminded him in a stronger voice. That wasn't so far from the truth. She was soaking wet. 'If you could get the power back on…' she suggested hopefully.

Marco narrowed his eyes and looked at her. 'You'd better take that bath,' he said, to her relief. 'And don't forget to reassure your godmother that you're safe. A storm like this will have made the international news. And anyone else, of course, who might be interested,' he added as an apparent afterthought.

He didn't fool her. 'There is no one else.' She guessed that was his real question. 'And I will speak to my godmother as soon as the phone line comes back.'

'You obviously think a lot of her.'

Passion and gratitude swept over her. 'My godmother is the most wonderful woman on earth. She took me in—'

'When your parents were killed,' Marco supplied thoughtfully.

'Yes.' She firmed her lips, reluctant to say anything more. How much did he know?

'Why did you leave her to come here to work in Tuscany?'

'It's a great job,' she said frankly. 'And I can't just live off her. She found this opportunity for me when I left my last job. She found it through one of her friends, another keen gardener. It would have been churlish of me to turn it down.'

Though maybe she should have done, Cass reflected as Marco continued to stare at her. He was beginning to make her nervous. She decided to give him a little more. 'I can easily get a job at another supermarket when I go home, and in the meantime this job is perfect for me.'

'Perfect,' Marco echoed without comment or expression.

He might want to know more, but she wasn't going to discuss her personal life with someone who was practically a stranger.

'Don't catch cold,' he reminded her.

She didn't need another prompt. She left him and ran across the courtyard without a backward glance. Racing up the steps to her room, she felt as if the devil was on her back.

He stood in silence when Cassandra left him. She had handled the crisis with impressive calm and now she intrigued him more than ever. Apparently uncomplicated and open, she was, in fact, as much a closed book as he was. He would like to find out more about her. She was hopeless at taking orders, but she was a breath of fresh air. Having worked closely with her, he now felt the lack of her, like a caged lion, penned in with a woman he wanted in his bed. He would be ill-advised to seduce her, he reminded himself firmly. He never slept with his employees.

He eased the physical ache with practicalities, starting up the generator and checking the garden to assess the damage. He huffed dryly to see her seedlings had survived when trees that had stood for centuries were lying broken on the ground. He should give her a long-term contract just to build drainage channels for him.

Having checked the sandbags were doing their job, he marvelled that she could lift them at all. He was trying to exhaust himself, he realised, in an attempt to put Cassandra out of his mind. That didn't stop his body craving her, or his mind from examining every tiny detail he knew about her. Cassandra Rich was the most unsettling woman he'd ever met. She was everything he would usually avoid. She was too young, too naïve, and she had no inkling of their relative positions in life—which was something else he liked about her, he now discovered. There were far too many toadies in his world. Cassandra Rich was real, he concluded with a shrug. If he were stranded in another storm, would he want Cassandra at his side or one of those fragrant types he usually went for? He'd choose Cassandra every time.

He laughed as he jogged up the stairs. There were so few surprises left in life, he almost welcomed her arrival into his remote, complex world.

So few surprises?

He was about to get the surprise of his life. He stopped dead on the threshold of his room. His window was closed, but his shutters were open and Cassandra's light was on.

She would never know what made her do it, other than to say she had seen pictures in magazines and films, as well as images in her head, of the type of sophisticated temptress a man like Marco would most likely be attracted to. That woman would be a minx, a siren, a temptress—all the things that capable Cass, as they had called her at the supermarket, most certainly wasn't. But there was nothing to stop her playing out her fantasy.

Perhaps it was the warmth of the evening and having a man like Marco close by and yet at a safe distance that had made exploring her own sexuality not just irresistible but an imperative. She'd missed having fun, but Tuscany seemed to have released something in her.

Working side by side with Marco had certainly released something in her, Cass reflected mischievously—and that was her excuse for dancing around the room while she waited for her bath to fill. In her dreams, she was dancing for him—and Marco was drooling, of course.

In reality, he wouldn't want his gardener, but what fun were bare facts? Her job here would end soon and he would be out of her life, but for now…let the dream continue!

Taking a breather, she went to peer out of the window. Marco's lights were safely off and his room was empty. Thank goodness! For a moment she had felt a rush of concern, wondering if he was watching her from the shadows. But no. It was just her and the moonlight, and she was safe to continue with part two of the show, dancing on her imaginary stage, beneath the moon, her imaginary spotlight…

He stood transfixed as Cassandra started to undress. She had her back to him, and was performing a slow and rather skilful striptease. When the top came over her head and he caught a glimpse of the ripe swell of her breasts, he was disappointed that the angle at which she was standing prevented him from seeing more. His imagination lost no time supplying the detail, and he groaned at the prospect of another night without sleep.

Allowing her top to drop to the floor, she removed the band from her ponytail and let her hair flow free in a shimmering cascade down her back. Running her fingers through it, she shivered a little as it fell around her shoulders, as if the touch of her hair on her naked skin aroused her. Still moving with a tantalising lack of haste, she freed the fastening at the waistband of her jeans, and reaching her hands behind her back she slipped her fingers beneath the denim, pushing it down over the swell of her hips. When she arched her back, it was almost as if she was presenting her buttocks for his approval. He did approve.

He went still as she stepped out of the jeans. Many women had tried to seduce him, and a good few had succeeded, but no one had made him feel as hungry as this. He was transfixed by the sight of Cassandra running her fingertips lightly over her breasts, her hands lingering, as if she appreciated the pertness of her nipples as much as he did. His senses roared as she pinched them. She appeared to cry out softly at the pain. Rolling her head back, she cupped her breasts and drew them forward as if inviting him to suckle. He would go mad if this went on for much longer.

He tensed as her hands travelled down over the swell of her belly. She had reached another place he would like to take his time exploring. She traced the swell lightly with her fingertips before delving deeper, and when she withdrew her hand he sucked in a noisy breath, only to realise that for the past few seconds he hadn't breathed at all. Cassandra had seemed so innocent, and yet these were the actions of a very sensual woman, who knew exactly how to torment a man. For all her physical strength and forthright manner, Cassandra was as lush and womanly as he could wish for. And, in the biggest surprise of the night, she had turned out to be the most erotically provocative female he'd ever met. He wondered if her pleasure was always self-administered. Her right arm was undulating lazily. Was she touching herself intimately? He had never been so aroused by the sight of a woman doing that. He was in agony.

What was she doing? Cass asked herself in shock, bringing a sudden halt to her performance.

She should be curled up safely in bed. She could only put her behaviour down to a release of tension now the storm had passed, and the old house she was coming to love had survived, because this was way over the top, and she had to stop doing it right now.

Had she lost her mind completely? She hadn't even closed the windows—

Grabbing the towel she'd laid ready for her bath, she secured it around her body, and then turned around to check that she hadn't been seen.

Marco's shutters were firmly closed, thank goodness.

Closed? Had they been closed before?

She couldn't remember. She could only remember thinking that his room had been in darkness. Maybe they had been closed. They must have been closed, she reassured herself sensibly.

CHAPTER FOUR

HE WAS TENSE at breakfast for obvious reasons. Cassandra, on the other hand, appeared to be totally relaxed, and was her customary rosy-cheeked self. After her assertiveness during the storm, and her astonishing striptease performance afterwards, she appeared to be as cool, calm and collected as ever.

'Sorry—didn't you want eggs again?' she asked him as he groaned out loud, thinking back to her dance in the moonlight.

'Eggs are good—eggs are fine. Thank you.' He sat back in his chair and tried to not to think about Cassandra and her night-time activities.

'My cooking skills are pretty basic,' she added, as she busied herself at the business end of the kitchen. 'Maria should get back today, so tomorrow you'll have better food.'

And then she bent down to put a pan away and her faded denim shorts clung tightly to the outline of her bottom. The urge to join her—to stand behind her and press his body into hers—to map her buttocks with one hand holding her in place, while he pleasured her with the other—

'More bread? Eggs? Coffee?' she called out.

'No. Thank you.'

When she turned to face him, his thoughts were not of

breakfast but of slowly sinking into her welcoming body and sheathing himself to the hilt. Her long, slender legs would wrap around his waist, and she would move with him. Her soft cries of need would urge him on, as he worked steadily to bring her release—multiple releases, he amended. He sat up as she put a hand to her forehead. 'Something wrong?'

'Dishwasher tablets!'

He blinked. 'I beg your pardon?'

'We're out of them,' she explained, frowning.

So much for his fatal charm! Though, far from being discouraged, her quirky ways had only fuelled his hunger for her.

Marco di Fivizzano was driving her crazy. He was about to start clearing the garden after the storm as she set out to go shopping, and he was stripped to the waist with an axe in his hand, looking like every one of her fantasies come true. But who was he, really? Her boss was so wealthy and powerful he could keep his backstory under wraps. That didn't stop her wondering about him. He made her curious. Everyone had an interesting backstory, once she had scraped the surface, but Marco didn't allow anyone to get close enough to tickle his back, let alone scrape his surface.

She wouldn't mind tickling his back… She wouldn't mind digging her fingers into those impressive shoulder muscles—

The spell broke abruptly as Maria came bustling out of the house. There had obviously been a call for Marco. Burying the axe in the tree stump, he led the way back into the house.

Sometimes life was so unfair, Cass mused wryly as

Marco and his delightful body disappeared inside the house. But there was always a next time…

She spent the afternoon in the village, where it was tranquil and cool after the storm. She still had some work to do in the garden to make sure everything was straight again, so she set off back to the house as soon as she could, and was surprised to find Marco pacing the kitchen, waiting for her.

'Leave that now,' he said, as she started to put away the shopping.

'What's wrong?' She frowned as she straightened up.

'We need to talk.'

She felt a frisson of alarm, and couldn't help wondering if she was about to lose her job. She couldn't bear to lose this job. It was perfect for her. It was her first step out of the shadows without having to confront a complex world. She had shunned the spotlight since escaping the tarnished glitter of her childhood, and here in Tuscany she was taking her first step back into the light.

'Come into my study,' Marco instructed.

His tone was stern, adding to her apprehension. She glanced around, thinking to learn something of him from this inner sanctum, but there was no clutter or ornament… no softening touches anywhere, as far as she could tell. There were no plants sunning on the windowsill, or papers left lying casually about. The room was still, and preternaturally tidy. It was also very expensively fitted out. He didn't invite her to sit down. She wouldn't have felt comfortable if he had.

He launched straight in. 'I've got a problem.'

'A problem?' For a moment her brain refused to compute the idea that Marco di Fivizzano could have any problem he couldn't solve, let alone a problem he was about to share with her.

'I need your help, Cassandra,' he elaborated, spearing her with one of his hard looks.

'What can I do for you?' Unless he was seeking advice on root propagation, or wanted to discuss soil management in a country that was basically a long piece of rock with almost unworkable clay loam soil, she couldn't think how she could help him. And she somehow doubted he'd brought her in here to talk about gardening.

'I've been let down.'

'Oh. I'm sorry.' Had she let him down? Was her dream job here about to shatter into a shower of tiny pieces?

'Not you,' he snapped impatiently.

Coming around to the front of his desk, he leaned back against it and folded his arms.

Narrowing his eyes, he looked down at her as if she were a cup cake amongst many in a cake shop window and he was trying to decide if she would do.

She didn't like that look in his eyes one bit, so she decided to seize the initiative. 'What can I do for you?'

Marco took his time replying, which gave her the chance to study him. Did he ever shave while he was in Tuscany? He really relaxed here. As she did.

She quivered with awareness, realising that his stare had dropped to her lips. She now realised that she had pursed them in an unintentionally sexy way. Quickly chewing the pout out of them, she straightened up and adopted a more businesslike manner.

'I need you in Rome.'

'In Rome?' She was jolted out of her trance in an instant. Rome—bustling, glittering, sophisticated. She couldn't go to Rome! But then another, far more calming thought came to her. 'You have a garden there?' Her heart soared at the thought of tending a city garden. It would be very different from here. She could imagine it would be enclosed and quiet, and an entirely different challenge from Tuscany. But a garden…that was something she could handle for him.

'It's nothing to do with gardens,' he rapped impatiently. 'I have a charity event I host each year.'

'I see,' she murmured, frowning. She didn't see at all. In fact, her mind was a blank canvas on which he could paint pretty much anything.

'It's a dinner,' he explained, as if she should know all about it. 'And I need a plus one, or there will be an empty space next to me.'

And that would be unthinkable, she silently supplied.

'The organiser of the charity was supposed to be my dinner partner,' he elaborated with an impatient gesture, 'but a family emergency has prevented that.'

'So, you'll have an empty seat next to you,' she said, frowning as if such things were a mystery to her.

'No. I won't,' Marco assured her, 'because you will be sitting in it.'

'Me?' Horror filled her. This was everything she had spent her adult life avoiding, and she had no intention of going to some glitzy party.

'I don't know why you sound so shocked,' Marco countered. 'I'm only inviting you to join me at a party.'

What the hell was wrong with her? Other women would be falling over themselves to accept this invitation, but not Cassandra. Oh, no. She was looking at him as if he had suggested some extreme and arcane form of torture—that, or a Roman orgy.

'A charity event in Rome? A dinner?' she confirmed, paling as she continued to frown.

'I don't know what's so hard for you to understand. Just say yes. I'll provide the clothes, the hairdresser, the manicurist. You'll have beauticians and stylists on tap—whatever you need.'

Her eyes widened, and then, to his astonishment, she said, 'You are joking?'

'I'm being perfectly serious.' Her reaction baffled him. 'I have just invited you to join me at the event of the year.'

'Well, I can't,' she insisted. 'I just couldn't do it. I couldn't pull it off,' she insisted, when he stared at her with incredulity. 'I'd be falling over the hem of my gown, knocking into people—'

'Hopefully not,' he said wearily.

'You are serious,' she added quietly, as if he had been speaking in a foreign language and she had only just worked it out. 'You want me at your side, at the top table at a charity event in Rome?'

'Yes. I do,' he confirmed. How many more times did he have to say it?

She shook her head. 'I'm really sorry, Marco, but the idea of me all tricked out in a gown and on my best behaviour is about as likely as you getting down and dirty in the garden.'

'But I do get down and dirty in the garden,' he reminded her, all out of patience now. 'Of course, if you're not up to this…'

Her heart was hammering in her chest. Marco had to be crazy—or desperate, asking her to do this. 'Thing is, I function best in a garden,' she explained firmly. 'I don't function at all at a…function.'

'I'd pay you for your trouble.'

That stopped her. 'You'd pay me? How much?' she said faintly, thinking of her godmother now.

Marco named a sum that drained the blood from her cheeks.

As he had expected, the mention of a large sum of

money turned the tide. Every woman had her price. But then Cassandra started stuttering something that sounded dangerously like no—and no was not an answer he could accept.

He turned up the pressure to put her back on track.

'What are you going to do when you leave here and go back to England? Will you work at the supermarket, stacking shelves?'

'Why not?' she demanded, showing no reaction to his scorn. 'It's honest work, and I've made some very good friends at the supermarket.'

'And you can make some very good friends in Rome,' he said, seething with frustration. 'Friends with fabulous gardens that need a lot of care and attention. You can network at the party, if nothing else.'

She blinked and appeared to reconsider. 'You'd introduce me round?'

He balked at that. 'Well, my people would. You'd get your money, and you'd get the chance to network. I don't see much wrong with that.'

And neither did she, from the look on Cassandra's face. His senses sharpened as she bit down on the full swell of her bottom lip while she considered his suggestion.

'I suppose—'

'You'll do it,' he said.

'I suppose if it will help—'

'It will help.'

'But I've only brought one dress with me—'

'I've told you,' he said, forcing patience into his tone. 'I will provide a dress for you to wear.'

'I'll pay you back.'

'The dress and all the other expenses will form part of your payment. You may keep the dress afterwards,' he added as a generous afterthought.

She hummed and frowned.

'You'll have everything you need,' he promised. 'I'll see to that.'

'And you're quite serious about this?'

'Cassandra, I never say anything I don't mean.'

He sat back, confident that this time she'd say yes.

'I need more time to think about it.'

'No,' he said flatly. 'You give me your answer now. Yes? Or no?'

She couldn't pretend she wasn't anxious at the thought of making a return to a shallow world of sophistication that had proved so damaging in her youth, but when she weighed that against the fact that the money Marco had offered would help to pay for her godmother's ticket to Australia. She knew it was a golden opportunity, and one that might never come around again.

She had to remind herself of this as she walked self-consciously into one of the most exclusive hotels in Rome. At the back of her mind she still had this nagging suspicion that Marco had bought her. But at least she could comfort herself with the thought that he had got the raw end of the deal. She was a gardener, not a socialite, and no number of designer gowns would change that.

But it was too late to worry about it now. She was here, with one of Marco's *people* shepherding her through the lobby.

She tensed as the hotel manager approached. The memories of her childhood had faded, but she was sure she had stayed in a place like this when she'd been a little girl. She couldn't remember her mother being around, but there had always been women. Her father had used women like commodities, and according to the press had possessed an animal magnetism that had made him irresistible. *Much like Marco.* In her father's case, this had led to serial infidelities that had broken her mother's heart.

She had vowed to stay away from this world, and yet here she was.

Cass swallowed convulsively as the manager bowed over her hand and smiled. She had to remind herself that this was all in a good cause, and that it would enable her to buy the ticket to Australia for her godmother.

'I hope you will be very happy here, *signorina*,' the hotel manager said with practised charm.

'I'm sure I will be,' she lied, for his sake. This was his hotel, and it was very beautiful. Located on one of the main streets in Rome, it was as discreetly labelled as the dress size of a couture gown. She knew quite a lot about couture gowns now, since her first stop of the day had been to the *atelier* of a designer who specialised in 'the style of gown Signor di Fivizzano favoured', according to Marco's *people*, who had arrived in a squad to take her in hand.

Atelier was a posh word for a workshop with a rather uncomfortable sitting room attached, she had discovered, as the designer measured every inch of her so he could prepare a toile, or pattern, from which any number of *visions*, as he called a frock, could be created.

Signor di Fivizzano might favour a particular style of gown, but she had made it clear from the off that if she didn't feel comfortable she wouldn't play the game. Plunging necklines and sausage skins were out. She didn't care how exclusive the fabric might be, the shape had to be right for her. The designer had shuddered at her mention of sausages, but he had promised to supply her with a rail full of his *visions* to choose from. That had taken up a great deal of time and the event was closing in. There was no time to lose, and so she made the best of things, pinning a smile to her face as the hotel manager led her forward.

'I'll leave you now,' Marco's man said briskly, according her a small bow. 'You'll have half an hour to settle in, and then your assistants will arrive.'

'My assistants?'

Too late! Having nodded briskly to the manager, Marco's man was on his way.

The manager's face was now a professional mask, devoid of all expression, but she had to wonder what he made of her in her one shabby dress—a sale rail number that had seemed a good idea at the time but which now, she realised, having just caught sight of herself in one of the mirrors in the lobby, made her look like a galleon in full sail. And as for the hideous pattern—

'Signorina?' he prompted with an almost balletic gesture. 'No expense has been spared,' he added approvingly as they waited for the elevator. 'Three hairdressers will attend you in our best suite—on the top floor.'

Three hairdressers? Was she a three-headed hydra?

Snake charmers this way, she thought dryly as the steel doors slid open.

They exited the elevator into a lobby discreetly decorated in tones of cream, taupe and ivory, with just a hint of Caligula in the crumbling Roman busts that lined the walls on marble plinths. She didn't need any more encouragement to shudder with a sense of impending doom.

'Your people will be with you shortly,' the manager announced, opening the door onto the suite with a flourish.

The suite was at least twice as big as her godmother's house. Picture windows overlooked Rome—towering antiquity existing happily alongside modernity—and it was a stunning view, but her mind was full of Marco. She only had to look at herself in the mirror to know how out of place she would be at his function, and how quickly he would realise his mistake. It would take more than a team of beauticians to put this right—she'd need a miracle.

And there was another thing—what man would spend this sort of money on a woman without expecting more than small talk? Fantasies were fine, but reality was something else with a man so potent and virile he made Genghis Khan look like a drooping weed. And she had far more sense than to get hot and heavy with her boss. She wanted to keep this job—

She jumped at a knock on the door. Swinging it wide, she stood back as her *team* filed in.

'Where is she?' a man with a lavender quiff demanded, staring about.

She pressed back against the door, quailing beneath his scrutiny. She could only imagine the many faults he would find with her.

Narrowing his mascaraed eyes, lavender quiff stared at her. 'Are *you* Signorina Rich?' He couldn't have sounded more horrified.

'I'm afraid so.' She smiled and jumped to attention.

Lavender quiff did not smile. Finely plucked brows rose at an improbable angle as he leaned in to examine her more closely. He almost, but not quite, managed not to groan.

'Well. We'd better get started,' he said, pursing his lips. 'I can see that I've got a lot to do.'

'What exactly are your instructions?' she asked, glancing around nervously as beauty professionals laid out what might be instruments of torture, for all she knew, along with an improbable quantity of make-up and scent.

Lavender quiff consulted his phone. 'Do what you can with her,' he intoned.

Marco clearly didn't expect too much of her. No pressure, then, Cass concluded wryly as she resigned herself to her fate.

CHAPTER FIVE

'AND THE GRAND REVEAL! Come on, sweetie, do try and put a good face on it,' lavender quiff, whom Cass now knew was called Quentin, pleaded as he heaved a theatrical sigh. 'The livelihoods of all these people depend upon you making a good impression at the party. And, believe me, they have definitely earned their money tonight.'

Cass laughed as Quentin took hold of her hands. He had relaxed her—and he had surprised her by turning out to be the best fun. Every time she had worried that she couldn't pull this off, Quentin had shaken her out of it. He was just the best at bolstering her confidence. With a purse of his lips, or a tweak of her hair, he'd made everything seem that it might be all right. This was one occasion when first impressions were most definitely wrong. Quentin had turned out to be a real fairy godmother.

'You look beautiful,' he said.

'Why don't I believe you?' She pulled a face.

'I have no idea,' he protested. 'Nigel? Mirror, please…'

The room felt silent and she was stunned.

'Well? Say something, sweetie,' Quentin prompted.

She couldn't. She was too full of emotion. She was normally so down to earth, and yet after years of trying to blank out the past she was seeing not herself, looking spruced up and almost passable in the mirror, but her mother instead. Had her mother felt like this—like a chicken being prepared for the feast? She could remember enough to know that her mother had tried so desperately hard to keep the interest of Cass's father, and that to do that she had been forced to compete with much younger groupies. How helpless she must have felt…

'Sweetie?' Quentin prompted anxiously. 'Are you okay?'

'I'm fine,' she said, lifting her chin and adding a smile. Quentin and his team had worked so hard that she owed it to them to put a good face on this. 'I can't thank you enough,' she said to him and to everyone else.

To her embarrassment and amazement people started clapping, until the whole room was ringing with applause.

'Well, I can't pretend it's been easy,' Quentin admitted with a sigh. 'But I suppose it's a mark of my genius that you've turned out as well as you have.'

Where the hell was she? He had waited long enough. He glanced at his watch and then at the door. The event was being catered at his penthouse in the centre of Rome. One hundred carefully selected sponsors were attending. They would be raising a lot of money for the charity tonight, and everything had to be perfect. Cassandra could not be late. They'd be sitting down to dinner soon, and it was unthinkable that he would have an empty place next to him.

His internal rant ended abruptly when Cassandra entered the room. Everyone stopped talking and turned to look at her. His mind blanked completely. She looked stunning. Where had that poise come from—that enchanting smile that lit up the room? He was more used to seeing her up to her elbows in mud, leaning on a pitchfork handle.

She saw him at once and smiled, but her eyes were wary as she darted a glance around the room. This was not her comfort zone, though she was a good actress and stepped forward with apparent confidence. Only he had seen the momentary falter in her step; everyone else was riveted by the sight of her. But why was she alone? Where were his people?

He felt protective suddenly, and held his breath as she walked towards him. It was then he realised that Cassandra didn't need anyone to escort her, and that she could hold everyone's attention without any effort at all.

'So you got here eventually,' he said curtly as she halted in front of him.

'Good evening to you too,' she murmured, extending her hand. 'I wasn't in a position to speed things up.' Lifting her chin, she held his stare steadily. 'I think I presented the beauticians with more problems than they had anticipated.'

He ground his jaw, admiring her even more for her honesty. 'I doubt that.'

'I'm sorry if I've kept you waiting,' she added. 'This sort of transformation takes a lot of time. Do you approve?'

Her concern on this point at least was genuine. Did he approve? So much he wanted to tell everyone to leave.

'You'll do,' he offered coolly. She looked magnificent. She looked like a queen—like a goddess, a fact that hadn't been lost on any man in the room.

'Do I look good enough?' she prompted, with real concern in her voice.

'Of course you do,' he said shortly. 'Can you really imagine Quentin setting you free unless he was completely satisfied?'

At last she laughed. 'I suppose not,' she confessed, smoothing her hands down her dress.

The gown was composed of some floating sky-blue fabric, cunningly cut to mould her ripe figure. He would give the designer a bonus on top of his extortionate fee for designing a dress so perfect for Cassandra. The shade of blue brought out the colour in her eyes, and while the neckline was higher than he would have preferred, maybe he was wrong in thinking it should be lower. As it was now, it hinted at the treasures underneath without revealing them. He found this more provocative than putting everything she had in such lush abundance on show.

The gown was sculpted so precisely it made him wonder if she had room for underwear beneath. His best guess was no.

And her hair— *Dio!* Her hair! Flowing free to her waist, it shimmered like a golden cape as it flowed in thick, glossy waves down her back—a back that was naked, he noticed as she turned around. The gown had been cut high at the front, yet it dipped practically to the swell of her buttocks at the back.

'Shall we sit down?' he suggested, feeling the need to get out of range of all the hungry male glances.

'Why not?'

Why not? Because he wanted to take her straight to bed.

Tonight was shaping up to be the most extreme form of torture he'd ever known. He led her to the table and pulled out her chair. He was determined to make her feel at ease, relaxation being a prerequisite for seduction.

He employed the best chefs in Rome and the food was delicious. Cassandra ate little at first, but he tempted her until she met his gaze and grinned. After that she relaxed enough to steal titbits from his plate. And she was charming to his guests. He'd never had a dining companion like her before. They usually took their lead from him—waiting for him to initiate a conversation or to introduce them to one of the other guests. Cassandra simply spread her natural charm about, and everyone, from the starchiest diplomat to the snootiest aristocrat, soon fell under her spell.

'You've hardly eaten anything,' she pointed out towards the end of the meal.

'I've been too busy watching you,' he admitted.

Her cheeks flushed red, and then she turned to answer a question from the guest on her other side.

Marco was looking at her in a way that made her body yearn for more than a bath and a good night's sleep. His eyes were so wicked and confident that it was becoming hard to remember why she was here, which was to be a seat-filler and not his companion. From mud to magnificent, she mused wryly as she surveyed the glittering throng. It still seemed incredible that one minute she had been in the garden and the next she was here—

'Would you like to dance?'

'What?' She stared at him stupidly.

'I said would you like to dance?' Marco repeated. 'More specifically, would you like to dance with me?'

Dance with Marco di Fivizzano? Was he mad? She had two left feet and a sense of rhythm to rival a rhino's. She had to quickly change her expression when she realised that she was staring at him open-mouthed as if he had suggested they have sex on the table.

'You do dance?' he pressed.

'I have been known to.' But on her own—most likely jigging along to the latest hit tune. This kind of dancing, though—the up close and very personal variety—she wasn't very good at that at all.

'We're the only people left at the table,' Marco pointed out, glancing around.

'And you're worried that people will talk if you don't dance with me?'

His lips slanted as he raised a brow.

Okay, so Marco wasn't worried what people thought, but maybe she was. She was happy to help out by chatting to his interesting guests, but anything more than that… She glanced down a table lit by legions of candles that cast a warm glow over the glittering crystal and silver. What was she doing here in Marco di Fivizzano's fabulous penthouse in the best part of Rome?

What would her mother think about it?

That she was holding a candle to the devil?

She felt a stab of pain, realising that she'd been too young when her mother had died to have a clue what she'd say.

'Just say yes,' Marco advised, standing up.

As he broke into her thoughts, she looked up blankly. If she remained seated, people would notice, and this event was for charity. So she stood and walked as if in a dream as Marco led her towards the dance floor. Anticipating his touch was stealing the breath from her lungs. When he actually touched her, she knew she might faint.

Don't be so ridiculous, she told herself firmly as he drew her into his arms. *It was the most amazing feeling...* But she had to look on this as a job with perks, and nothing more.

'Relax.' He laughed softly in her ear, making a tingle race down her spine as he added, 'I can't dance with a board.'

'And I can't dance with you at all. I did warn you.' She definitely couldn't—shouldn't be dancing with a man who made her feel like this. She was bound to trip over her dress or step on his feet—

'I'll lead,' he murmured, as if there was any doubt.

The next moment her body was moulded to his—her body had a mind of its own, as she'd noticed since arriving in Tuscany, but it wasn't long before the music wooed her. Marco wooed her. Pressing her close against his iron-hard frame, he seduced her into dancing with him, while the melody soothed her, reminding her of so many happy days in Tuscany. It wasn't hard to dance with him at all. The Italian music was just so beguiling. It had a charm all its own…

'You're a good dancer,' he said.

No one was more surprised than she was by that comment, but when he added, 'You should dance more,' he sent tremors of excitement racing through her.

But then she reasoned, who was she going to dance with—and where? Marco surely didn't mean she could dance with him—on what occasion? But what could possibly compare with this? She would never dance with another man again, because it could only be a disappointment after Marco.

This was turning into a magical night, and a magical occasion, and she was going to make the most of it, because she knew deep down that it would never happen again.

And then one of the sponsors asked if he could cut in. Marco stopped dancing and smiled. 'It would be ungracious of me to keep you all to myself,' he explained. 'Do you mind if I allow the ambassador to dance with you?'

'You? Allow?' she queried softly, out of the ambassador's hearing, she thought, but the ambassador had overheard, and he laughed.

'It appears that this young woman knows you, Marco. And quite right, my dear. It's up to you to choose your partner,' he added, smiling at her warmly.

'Then I would love to dance with you,' she said as she slipped out of Marco's arms.

When she started dancing with the ambassador, she

noticed Marco watching her. It might not be sensible, but she liked that he was watching her.

He had grudgingly—very grudgingly—given way to the ambassador. He missed having Cassandra in his arms. He missed the warmth of her soft body pressed up close to his.

He was paying the woman to be here, he reminded himself. He should not mistake this for anything more—though there was nothing to stop him enjoying her company while they were in Rome.

He could tolerate the older man dancing with her, but when one of the younger sponsors tried to cut in, he returned to the dance floor and reclaimed her.

'Excuse us, Ambassador. I'm sure you'll understand.' He didn't care if the man understood or not. Cassandra was coming with him. 'The auction is about to start soon. Cassandra?' he prompted.

She looked daggers at him, though she was charm personified to the ambassador, who was a courtly old man and hadn't deserved his rough treatment. 'I apologise for denying you the company of this young woman,' he felt bound to add, brought to book by the piercing stare of his assistant gardener. He had to do some serious thinking on that front, but as the auction was about to start…

'I quite understand,' the ambassador told him, with a look that said he did—absolutely. 'I'll see you again someday, my dear, I hope.'

'I hope so too,' she said, with what even he had to admit was a lovely smile.

'There are some wonderful things in the auction,' Cassandra told him with enthusiasm as soon as they were seated back at the table.

Of course, he thought. All the items on sale were unique

and extremely valuable, in order to raise as much money as possible for the charity.

'Have you seen something you like?' Placing a bid was the least he could do when she had worked so hard to charm his guests.

'As a matter of fact, I have,' she said.

'Tell me,' he prompted indulgently.

'It's that lovely sketch of a dachshund puppy—the Hockney? In my fantasies, I imagine taking it home for my godmother as a gift. Don't worry,' she said before he had chance to say a word. 'I know they fetch tens of thousands, hundreds, probably—maybe millions by now—but it doesn't cost to dream.'

They both knew that works by the artist David Hockney could go for a fortune. All the auction lots would go for fabulous amounts of money, their value further increased by the fact that they were being sold for charity. Part of him wanted Cassandra to bid—he'd cover any amount she went to. But what would that say to the watching world?

Surprising himself, he covered her hand with his, as if to reassure her. Tender gestures were not his thing, but there was something about Cassandra…

CHAPTER SIX

THE BIDDING WAS over and everyone had left the table. Most of the charming older people had left, Cass discovered when she scanned the glamorous main salon. The networking she'd planned to do wasn't so easy when the people who were left behind didn't want to talk to her, and those who had gone were too nice to touch up for a job. She had just wanted to talk to them and enjoy their company.

Spotting Marco across the room, she thought now might be a good time to ask him to introduce her round. But, contrary to his earlier, sympathetic manner, when she had lusted after the Hockney sketch, his back was like a wall against her when she turned up, as if he regretted his brief display of almost being human, and was once again the aloof billionaire, untouchable and cold.

She hovered for a little while, uncertain. People moved around her as if she weren't there… She wished she wasn't there. This was a world she had avoided and had no desire to become part of again—a world where people said one thing and did another.

She moved into the shadows of a corner where she could observe, without being observed, and that was how, in a brief lull in the general conversation, she heard Marco say, 'That girl in the blue dress, sitting next to me at dinner? She's no one.'

Shock chilled her, but what he'd said was true. She wasn't anyone—not compared to all these rich and influential people. She was an amateur gardener—an enthusiast who had taken a summer vacation job on Marco di Fivizzano's country estate. When she returned home, she would be back stacking shelves at another supermarket.

Hearing Marco say what he had was actually a welcome wake-up call. She had nothing in common with anyone here. She must have been mad to think she could network.

But then her fiery nature kicked in. What he'd said was true, but he shouldn't have said it to another guest. How would Marco like it if she had dismissed him like that?

Working her anger out, she kept on moving around his guests without stopping to talk to anyone. She'd lost her confidence to speak to anyone, thanks to him. Finally, locking herself in the bathroom, she stared at the face of a stranger in the mirror—a woman with false eyelashes and rouged cheeks…an actress playing a part.

Exactly. She was playing a part. And therefore she could do this. Even if she was no one, on a scale of ambassador to prince, she could still hold her head high and go back to the party to do exactly what she'd been paid for.

And that was what she did. She guessed that the same driver who had brought her here would take her back to the hotel, and meanwhile, as the last guests began to think about leaving, she set about doing what she could to tidy up. She had always felt compelled to tidy up, maybe because the last time she had seen her mother alive, her mother had been stumbling about amidst the squalor of spilled ashtrays, discarded needles and upended champagne bottles. Since then Cass could never leave the debris of the night before until the next morning.

'What the hell are you doing?'

She froze as Marco roared at her. And then she fired

up. His manner was insufferable. Why had he paid her to come here at all? She was a member of his staff, and she saw no reason why she couldn't make a start on tidying up.

'Leave it!' he insisted. He was at her side in a couple of strides. 'I have staff to do this.'

'Are you going to make them work through the night?' she demanded, shaking his hand from her arm.

'Of course not,' he exploded.

The last thing he had expected was for her to answer back, Cass suspected as they glared at each other.

'My staff will be here in the morning,' Marco informed her brusquely.

And meanwhile they were alone…the last guest had left. And so far there was no sign of Marco's driver.

'What are you so angry about, Cassandra?'

She wasn't angry. She had just realised the compromising position she had put herself in. 'You think you can insult me and I won't feel anything?'

'Insult you? What on earth are you talking about?'

'You,' she fired back. 'You talk about your staff as if they're robots programmed to obey. You promised to introduce me round. You said it would be a great opportunity for me to network, and I thought so too, but you ignored me all night. I'm not sure why I'm here at all.'

'There were plenty of opportunities for you to network. It was up to you to take them. Everyone was here.'

'Everyone in your world,' she pointed out, 'and though I'm usually quite good at chatting to people and introducing myself, they just didn't want to know. An introduction from you would have broken the ice…' She paused. 'Or was it that you didn't want anyone to know you had brought your lowly gardener to the party?'

'Don't be so ridiculous. What about the ambassador?

You were talking to him. The embassy has beautiful gardens. There was an opportunity for you right there.'

'I was chatting to the ambassador because I wanted to talk to him. He was a really interesting man. Should I have taken advantage of that? Was I supposed to ingratiate myself with him for no better reason than to persuade him to give me a job?'

'Why not?' Marco demanded with a dismissive gesture. 'That's what networking is all about.'

'In that instance, it would have been calculating, and not very nice.'

'That's your opinion.'

'Yes, it is.'

'It's possible to be too nice, Cassandra.'

'Is it? Is it really? I had no idea there was such a thing as being *too* nice. I liked the ambassador. We got on well together, and I had no thought of using him for networking, as you suggest.'

'He could have given you a glimpse into another world—'

'As you can?' she flashed. 'Maybe I don't want to see what's in that other world—maybe I already know. You've got no idea, have you, Marco? You live such a privileged life you don't have a clue what it's like to be on the outside, looking in.'

'You couldn't be further from the truth,' he assured her tensely. 'I know exactly how that feels.'

'Do you?' she exclaimed angrily. 'Do you also know how it feels to be described as a nobody?'

Marco's expression blackened 'Who said that?'

'You did!' she flung back at him. 'Is that how you think of everyone who works for you? Are we all nobodies?'

'I have no idea what you're talking about.'

'I heard you say it.' And when Marco looked at her

blankly, she spelled it out for him. 'When one of your guests asked you about me, you said I was no one.'

'Ah…' Marco nodded his head. 'Let me explain. The man I was talking to was a major fundraiser for my charity. He's always on the lookout for new sponsors, as he should be—'

'And, of course, I'm no use to him. I couldn't do anything practical to help your charity, could I, Marco? And what can you do? Write another cheque?'

She had a point, he conceded. 'I'm sure you could do a lot for my charity, and if my shorthand way of telling a fundraiser that he was wasting his time asking you for money has offended you, I apologise. Maybe you shouldn't be so touchy.'

She shrugged. Her face was burning. Maybe she had overreacted.

'I agree that I'm no one where the funding side of your charity is concerned, but I could do other things apart from giving money. I could give my time, for instance.'

'I have no doubt of it,' Marco said, and then he surprised her with the hint of a smile.

It was the fact that they came from two such different worlds that was at the heart of her anger, Cass realised. Marco's world frightened her because she'd had experience of it, and, however many years ago it had been, there were some memories that never faded.

And Marco? Sometimes, when he relaxed like this and showed her a warmer, more caring side, she knew that his pain cut as deep as hers—he was just better at hiding it. They had never really talked, so she didn't know what lay behind Marco's armour. Why would they talk? She was paid to do a job. She was his gardener, briefly on an outing to help him. She was a place-filler, a puppet. 'You must think I'm stupid, overreacting like that…'

'Not at all,' he said firmly.

'But I am naïve enough to allow you to dress me up like a doll, and then expect you to be interested enough to spend all evening with me.'

'You are an extremely forthright woman,' he remarked with amusement in his eyes.

'Yes, I am,' she agreed.

'You did well tonight.'

'Are you mocking me now?' she asked suspiciously.

'No,' Marco murmured, the faint smile still in place. 'I'm very grateful to you. I can't think of anyone who could have pulled this off with such style and grace at such short notice. I'm only sorry I didn't make more effort to…break the ice for you, as you put it. I do know that society here can be very hard to break into.'

Cass slanted a rueful smile. 'And, I suppose, in fairness, your guests hadn't come here tonight to interview staff for their gardens.'

'I should have thought of that,' Marco admitted.

'And so should I.'

'Then we both got carried away.'

His eyes were deeply unsettling as they stared steadily into hers.

'Yes, we did,' she said.

'Truce?' he said.

'Truce,' she agreed, shaking hands with him.

Oh, how good that felt. She was almost disappointed when he let go and moved away.

'I've got something for you,' he said, turning back to her with a smile.

'Something for me?' She couldn't have been more surprised. 'You've paid me more than enough.' But she couldn't pretend she wasn't thrilled at the idea of a small gift—something personal from Marco. She'd keep it always, and long after this night was a memory she would find it and look at it, and think, *He gave it to me...*

'Oh, my word!' She couldn't have been more shocked. 'What have you done?'

'Please allow me, just this once, to fulfil someone's fantasy.'

She stared at the Hockney sketch in amazement. 'But this must have cost you a fortune.'

'In spite of what you think of me, I do value things in more than just monetary terms. You said you wanted this for your godmother. Well, now you can give it to her.'

'I can't possibly accept,' she protested.

'It's not for you, it's for her. You must accept,' Marco said.

'I don't know what to say.'

'Well, I do. She must be a very special woman.'

'She is.'

Marco was still staring at her with eyes turned thoughtful, while her head was muddied with feelings—too many feelings. A few more tense seconds passed, and then, just when she had found the words to form a polite refusal, she saw something flare in his eyes, and the next moment she was in his arms, and Marco was kissing her.

Her world had telescoped into this. Her world was this. Shocked, she resisted him for barely a moment before her body overruled her mind. This explosion of feeling and super-awareness was the very best way to end an argument, though seeing Marco every day and weaving fantasies around him had no bearing on the wealth of sensation flooding her now. He smelled—tasted—felt so good. She had never experienced anything like it. Being pressed up hard against his muscular frame, and having his arms tighten around her, was impossible to describe…not in words; only her body could respond with a burning desire to have not one fragment of space between them.

Breaking free, she was focused and breathless as she stood on tiptoe, pushing his jacket from his shoulders. She had to feel more of him—all of him. The sound of fabric ripping told her that her exquisite blue dress was a *vision* no more.

And now Marco's mouth was on her shoulder, claiming her, kissing her, licking and biting as he drew a cry from her throat by turning to rasp his sharp stubble across her neck. She was crying and laughing at the same time, while her hands worked with real purpose to tug off his clothes. Having managed to open his shirt, she gasped to see the power in his chest, the muscles flexing. He was so hard and tanned, and he was hers to explore.

Passion was running high between them as she ran the palm of one hand over his hot, smooth flesh. He dragged a cry from her throat, taking advantage of this brief distraction to cup her breasts. And he wasn't done with her yet. Taking hold of what was left of the fabric, he ripped her dress from neck to hem.

She was reduced to the flimsiest of underwear. This consisted of little more than flesh-coloured net that revealed every contour of her body in absolute detail. Looking down, she saw her rose-tinted nipples extended impertinently for his appreciation, and the soft mound between her legs, swollen and moist. If she had drawn this scene in one of her fantasies, she might have imagined feeling uncertain, standing practically naked in front of such a sophisticated lover, but the heat in Marco's eyes and the touch of his hands gave her confidence.

'I'm going to pleasure you,' he growled, angling his chin to stare into her eyes. 'I'm going to make you beg for more.'

'Okay.'

Throwing his head back, he laughed at her forthright acceptance of his offer.

Let him laugh. She had no intention of being a docile partner. She had needs too.

Smoothing the palms of her hands across the width of his shoulders, she removed his shirt and let it drop to the floor. Then she turned her attention to the buckle on his belt, and after that his zipper. She held his stare as she pushed his black silk boxers down over his taut, hard, muscular buttocks. Cupping them briefly, she indulged herself for a moment, before studying his erection. Thick and smooth, it was standing almost perpendicular, and her body ached to have him deep inside her. But Marco was the master of delay. Capturing her wrists, he pinned them behind her back, holding her still for him, while his other hand conducted a lazy exploration. Still staring her in the eyes, he protected them both, ripping the foil with his teeth. Anticipation was part of his foreplay, she gathered—and it was working, she would be the first to admit.

Cupping her breasts, he stroked them and weighed them appreciatively. He teased her nipples until she thought she'd go mad. Every part of her was responding eagerly to his touch, allowing her to sink into a rich velvet pool of sensation.

Frustratingly, Marco kept a space between them, although he did allow her to feel the brush of his erection. And then he touched her. But too lightly. And his hand never lingered long enough to satisfy her needs. And all this time he was smiling down at her, as if he knew exactly how frustrated he was making her.

She'd had enough and broke free.

Their tussle went up a notch. They were both determined to have the upper hand, and of course she couldn't fight him, but wrestling Marco was so much fun, and only added to her arousal. She rubbed her body against his—she rubbed every part of her against him. He seemed amused by her strength but she'd been working outdoors for weeks and had never been a weakling, but she would never be strong enough to dominate Marco.

That made it more fun. One minute he would let her think she was strong enough, and the next he would master her. Right now he had her in a firm hold and was tormenting her at his leisure. She tried calling him names, but it only made him laugh.

'You love it,' he said.

She would never admit to that, but he was right. Marco's expression, his wicked smile, and even the blinding flash of his strong white teeth—she loved everything about him.

'Do you think you can fight me?' he said.

'I know I can,' she hissed back.

She shivered, exultant when he slipped his hand beneath her flimsy bra. She thought for a moment that he was going to rip it off, but still he kept her waiting. The master of arousal had her in the firmest of grips, and he allowed her no choice other than to accept the pleasure he was dealing her. He stroked her breasts with the lightest of touches, and then had the nerve to smile when she whimpered with frustration. When she was least expecting it, he slipped his fingers beneath the delicate join holding the fragile cups of her bra together and ripped them apart. His eyes flashed with triumph when she cried out with surprise. Disposing of the ruined bra, he tossed the remnants aside, before turning his full attention to her breasts.

Now she could only breathe and exist as Marco touched her. He had robbed her of the power to do more. It wasn't just that he was holding her so she couldn't move while he pleasured her—it was more that she didn't want to move. Why fight pleasure? Wasn't it better to relax into sensation such as this, and enjoy?

She exclaimed with delighted shock when he pinched her nipples, and the sensation travelled rapidly around her body. She rested in Marco's arms, a willing victim to his skill—so much so that when he finally took hold of the waistband of her thong, she exclaimed with relief. She should have known he was still teasing her. Tracing the tiny scrap of lace around her waist, he slipped his fingers down between her buttocks, before returning to trail them across the swollen mound that was aching for his attention.

'More?' he suggested, angling his chin to shoot her a look with those wicked eyes.

She garbled something, which was all she could do. In answer, Marco cupped her with his hand, though with a touch so light it was even more frustrating than not being touched at all. With a growl of frustration she arched her back and thrust herself firmly against his hand, and then she worked her body shamelessly against it in the hunt for more contact, more pleasure…

'You have to tell me what you want, Cassandra.'

Marco's tone was deliciously stern. 'You.' She blazed a frank and fiery stare into his eyes. 'I want you.'

'And where do you want me?' he said calmly.

'Deep inside me.'

Before the words were out of her mouth Marco had lifted her arms above her head. Ramming her back against the wall, he held her in place with the weight of his body. Catching hold of her buttocks, he encouraged her to lift her legs and wrap them around his body as tightly as she could. She was happy to do so. She was claiming him. He wasn't going anywhere.

Lacing her fingers through his strong black hair, she

kept him close with their mouths just a fraction apart. His fierce stare burned into hers, but he refused to kiss her.

She thought she knew why. Marco didn't want her to close her eyes. He wanted to see everything she was feeling reflected in their depths. He wanted that degree of control over her, and that level of contact between them, when he took her for the first time. She wanted that too. She wanted to see Marco's responses just as hungrily as he wanted to see hers.

CHAPTER SEVEN

'NOW?' MARCO SUGGESTED softly, his mouth tugging a little at one corner as if he were mocking her need. Before she had a chance to answer, he tested her, and parting her with the tip of his erection he slid slowly and steadily into her until he was lodged deep, to the hilt.

'You're so tight…so wet…' he murmured appreciatively over her grateful moans.

And he was so big. She gasped with delighted shock, and then Marco worked some magic with his hand, and she was reduced to wordless sounds of need and pleasure. She was just building to an exciting climax when he withdrew completely. She had no sooner voiced her complaint with a cry and with fingers digging cruelly into his shoulders than he drew his hips back and thrust deep. Holding on was impossible. She fell gratefully into a series of violent pleasure waves. He didn't wait for her to quieten. Lifting her, he walked with her across the room where he lowered her down on the sofa. Standing over her, he spread her legs wide over his shoulders. 'Well?' he said with the faintest of smiles.

'Hard and fast?' she suggested.

Breath shot out of her in a noisy rush. Marco had taken her at her word, but nothing could have prepared her for this.

They made love all night in every part of the penthouse. They had hungry sex, fierce sex, and even playful sex, and there wasn't a surface they didn't sample. Their appetite for each other proved inexhaustible, and when she finally fell asleep in Marco's bed, it was with a happy smile on her lips and more contentment in her heart than she could ever remember feeling.

He woke at dawn and his first thoughts as always were centred around his work. He rolled out of bed and glanced at Cassandra. She was sound asleep. She had proved to be every bit as enthusiastic about sex as he had imagined. But that was all it had been, he told himself.

His mother had lived a lie for the sake of hooking up with a wealthy man. He would not be making that sort of mistake any time soon. The man he thought of as his father was a man his mother had tricked into marrying her, in order to provide her with an income stream and a father for her unborn child. Cassandra had briefly made him question his belief that women couldn't be trusted, but when he recalled the damage a woman could do, it was easy to shut down his emotions.

After his shower, he went into his dressing room and emerged ready for the day. Cassandra was just waking… stretching her limbs like an indolent cat. The image she presented—naked and lush, and so obviously sated—was quite different from her common-sense self in Tuscany.

'Marco…' She reached out a hand as if the effort was almost too much for her. 'Come back to bed…'

He frowned, and then realised that some words were necessary if he wasn't to appear wholly inconsiderate, but the affection and reassurance that Cassandra seemed to be asking for was beyond him.

'That was great, *cara*…' Walking over to the bed, he

dipped down to brush a kiss against her cheek. 'But I have to go now.' Leaving her side, he paused at the door. 'I left your money on the table in the hall…'

Her money?

For a moment Cass couldn't understand what Marco had said, and then she remembered that she was to be paid for filling a seat at his party, and that it was the money she could use to send her godmother on the dream trip.

That didn't make her feel any better. Sitting up in bed, she hugged herself, wishing that Marco's arms were around her, and that he was cuddling and reassuring her. She had wanted to tell him how much last night had meant to her. But now…

Scrambling out of bed, she dragged a sheet with her to wrap around her naked body. Crossing to the window, she waited until Marco had left the building, and then she watched him step into his car. She felt empty inside. As with everything else in his charmed life, Marco's trip to the office would be seamless. He wanted sex. He had sex. He wanted the car. The valet brought it to the door for him. No interruptions were allowed to the busy billionaire's schedule. Tenderness or a few moments of humour were beyond him—unless he was in seduction mode.

Blinded by tears, she turned around, furious with herself for being so stupid. Last night had been special for her, and she had thought it had meant something to him.

She took a long, hot shower in the hope that it would stop her shaking. She felt cold to the bone, and sick at the thought that Marco hadn't treated her much better than a prostitute. After paying for her services, he had all but ignored her at the charity function—but he hadn't ignored her when everyone had left. Then he'd been different, then he'd been interested—very interested indeed. And she was the fool who had allowed it to happen.

Ignoring her scattered clothes, the ripped reminders of an explosive passion that hadn't lasted the night, she pulled on the same frock she'd arrived in. Thank goodness Marco or his staff had had the foresight to have her things sent on from the hotel to Marco's penthouse. Scraping her hair back, she didn't bother with make-up. Why would she? Who would notice? Picking up the phone, she checked on flights home to England and then booked a cab to the airport. She'd got enough money to fly home, and there was no point in staying—not on Marco's terms.

Just thinking about it made her so angry she had to blink back tears. She had never been a victim, and she wasn't about to start now. When things went wrong, she did something about it.

When the cab driver called to say he was outside, she checked around one last time to make sure she'd got everything—and then stopped, frozen to the spot, at the sight of Marco's cheque on the hall table. She picked it up and studied the amount. She studied the bold script of Marco's signature. She couldn't imagine what he'd been thinking when he'd come up with such a ridiculous amount, let alone what she had been thinking when she'd accepted it. There was enough money here to send her godmother around the world first class with money to spare. A second call from the cab driver distracted her.

'Coming now,' she answered.

'Cassandra…Cassandra?'

He stared around the empty penthouse. Where the hell was she? He had expected a welcome, a smile, and a whole lot more. Was she still in bed? He felt a buzz of anticipation as he went to find out.

The buzz didn't last long. His room was empty, the bed neatly made. He knocked on the bathroom door…

Nothing.

He checked inside to be sure.

He searched the whole place, but it was silent and empty. There was no sign of her—no clothes on the floor, nothing out of place, not even a scribbled note to indicate where she had gone. And he'd distinctly told her to expect him later. He went back to the hallway where he'd left her cheque beneath a plant pot on the console table. *Where she couldn't have missed it.*

His cheque was still there.

He thought about calling her on his phone and then changed his mind. She must have gone back to the hotel. He dialled the number and reeled at the information that the receptionist gave him. Signorina Rich had called by to pick up her passport and suitcase *on her way to the airport.*

She'd left him?

He huffed a humourless laugh. Maybe it was for the best that she'd gone. The strength of his desire for Cassandra was warning enough to end it now. He would have done, if she hadn't gone.

But she'd gone.

Dio! He was her employer. She couldn't just walk out on him.

Striding across the room, he snatched up the cheque. Gripping it in his fist, he rang his PA. 'Find her.'

'Yes, sir.'

He slammed down the phone, refusing to accept that a small part of him couldn't let Cassandra go—not completely.

Cass made sure she wasn't easy to find. Her experience in Tuscany had bruised her. Bought and paid for like her mother, she was determined that she would not suffer the same fate. No one knew better than she did that a clean break with the past was the only chance anyone had to move forward. The person she had been in Rome wasn't her. Or, rather, it wasn't the person she wanted to be. She was Cass, plain and simple—not some glittering socialite with a rampant sex life, who stayed the night with the boss in order to keep him sweet.

Not everything was doom and gloom. Her godmother had flown to Australia to join her son, explaining that he had sent the fare for her, and, on Cass's recommendation, she had rented out her house to bring in some extra cash while she was away.

This was just the opportunity Cass had needed to quit the address Marco's people held on file for her and start over. She got a job at another supermarket, which paid just enough money to rent a small house in a nearby village. Her new home was tiny, but she loved it. She had put up a notice in the local post office, offering her services as a gardener, and to her surprise she was soon fully booked. With that and her work on the tills she was almost too busy for regret—until the day she fainted on the job, and an elderly lady she was serving asked her if she was pregnant…

'No. Of course not,' she protested, laughing at the absurdity of the question. 'What makes you think that?' But even as she spoke, a spear of alarm stabbed deep.

'A strong, healthy girl like you has no reason to feel faint—unless you're ill, which I doubt. I've had six children myself,' the old lady confided, 'so I know the signs.'

'I'm sure you're wrong…'

Cass tried to laugh it off, while all she wanted to do was to leave the store and rush to the pharmacy to pick up a pregnancy test, but she had to wait until she finished work.

It was the longest working day of her life. Back home, she stared at the test in shock. The thin blue line didn't lie, according to the instructions. But Marco had used protection, so how could this happen?

Quite easily, those same instructions informed her as she scanned the printed sheet.

No protection is foolproof.

Well, they'd got that right, and she was the fool.

'A call from Signorina Rich?'

Marco sat back in his leather seat, staring out across the majestic skyline of Rome. His secretary knew never to interrupt him unless it was to announce his next appointment, or unless it was a matter of vital importance, so Cassandra must be kicking up a fuss. The lack of her pained him, but the fact that she had walked out on him without a word had ended it as far as he was concerned. How long had it been now? Almost three months? What was so important she had to call him at the office? Had she changed her mind about the cheque?

'I have a ten o'clock meeting,' he snapped, frowning.

He drew breath to give himself a chance to weigh up the facts. Cassandra was back in his life, asking to speak to him. He needed to think about this for a few moments.

Calm reason triumphed. They hadn't expected to hear from each other. When something was over it was over, as far as he was concerned.

'Tell Ms Rich I'm too busy to take her call, but I'm happy to send her cheque on.'

Thoughts of Cassandra plagued him for the rest of the day, and flashbacks kept him from his work. These were not just of Cassandra, but of the past. Maybe because their pasts were quite similar he was thinking back to that frozen Christmas Eve when the man he had called *Papa* had thrown him and his mother out on the street, cutting them off without a penny or a word of farewell.

His mother must leave with nothing, the man he had thought was his father had instructed. That was the price of betrayal. More disillusionment followed when his mother had explained that *Papa* wasn't his father, and that the man who had fathered him had been an odd job man around the house, and now that man was gone too.

Even though their circumstances had been much changed, to begin with the two of them had rubbed along well enough. His mother hadn't been a fool, but the unrelenting hardship of their new life had eventually ground her down, and she'd begun to drink to blot it out.

Cassandra's mother had been a drunk too, so Cassandra knew how it felt when a mother chose to lose herself in a bottle of liquor, rather than care for her child.

When his mother had died he had found ways to make himself useful—carrying trash for restaurants in return for a good feed and carting logs for the rich folk who could afford them. He had vowed that one day *he* would go to school, and one day *he* would be rich.

And Cassandra?

She had been cast adrift in just the same way, and she was a survivor too.

With a frown of impatience he got back to his work and vowed not to allow thoughts of Cassandra to distract him. He relied on no one. He shared his past with no one. He never had. He couldn't afford this sort of disturbance to his working day. There must be no more calls from Cassandra.

'Your ten o' clock appointment is here, sir…'

'Thank you. Send him in.'

Closing the book on Cassandra Rich, he turned his attention back where it belonged, to the business that had never let him down.

* * *

Precious time was passing and Marco was still refusing to take her calls. Soon it would become obvious that she was pregnant, and he had to know. She had called her godmother in Australia and, typically, her godmother had shared Cass's delight. She had asked who the father was, and when Cass had enthusiastically said she'd be doing this alone, her godmother had immediately offered to come home. Cass had had to insist that this wasn't necessary, and had pointed out that her godmother's time with her son was precious. Cass had friends around, as well as the best of medical care, and she promised to get in touch with regular updates.

Marco's refusal to speak to her was one difficulty she had no intention of burdening her godmother with, Cass thought as she placed yet another call to Fivizzano Inc. She was tired of speaking to the same PA and receiving the same firm, but polite answer: 'I am sorry, *signorina*, but Signor di Fivizzano cannot take your call. He's too busy today.'

She would have to be back at the supermarket for her lunchtime shift in ten minutes, Cass realised, glancing at her phone. She had called Marco every day at different times of day, hoping that eventually she'd be put straight through to him. She still couldn't believe that she'd slept with such a cold-hearted man—or that she had never asked for his private number, but there was no point in regretting that now.

The same PA picked up, and Cass received the same stock answer, but this time she interrupted before the PA had a chance to hang up. 'I'm sorry…did you say Signor di Fivizzano is too busy to speak to me?'

'That is correct, *signorina*. I do apologise—'

'He wasn't too busy to sleep with me.' She paused—

not that she needed to as the silence was crushing. 'He wasn't too busy to make me pregnant. Could you tell him that, please? Thank you,' she added politely before she cut the line.

Sitting back, she firmed her chin. The die had been cast. She'd done her part. She wanted nothing from Marco in the material sense, but it was her duty to let him know. What he did next was up to him. What she did next would be all about her baby's future.

He didn't say a word when his red-faced PA recited Cassandra's call back to him, but his mind was racing.

'Thank you.' His curt nod of the head revealed nothing of the turmoil inside him.

A child?

He had given life to a child?

How could that have happened when he was always so careful?

Had he been so careful that night? Hadn't he been out of control for the first time in his adult life...because of Cassandra, and the way she had made him feel?

He was never out of control. He was confident on that point. But had he been as meticulous as he usually was when it came to using protection? They had indulged so many times it was hard to be certain. He had been consumed by a fever of lust and so had she. He'd never known anything like it, which made her behaviour afterwards—leaving him without a word of explanation—all the harder to understand. Until he brought up the past and put what he'd learned from it into the equation.

This ruse had been used before, he remembered, getting up to pace the floor—false pregnancies, floods of tears, women trying to tell him that it was better without using protection, and *of course they were on the Pill*. Not one of those women had been telling the truth. He'd had them all investigated. There were no babies, just dishonest women looking for an easy ride.

Did that sound like Cassandra?

He didn't want children. Why would he, with his history?

Could he find feelings? Could he buy them? Since learning that he'd been unwanted, he had learned not to care. He'd been doing that for too long now to change, and a child needed more. A child needed everything.

He struggled with the thought that Cassandra had done this on purpose to secure a meal ticket, like other women, like his mother. But was he the father of her child? Cass hadn't been a virgin when he'd met her. How could he be sure?

He couldn't go on like this. Thoughts of Cassandra were interfering with his life. He'd have to ring and have it out with her.

In a trick that only fate could play on him, he discovered she had changed her number.

Don't you trust your own judgement? Cassandra is different from all those other women. Have you forgotten that so easily?

The past vied uncomfortably with what he knew about Cassandra. She wasn't weak. She wasn't greedy. She had never asked him for anything. It was he who had pressed things on her—the dress, the makeover, the sketch, and then the cheque.

He called the team that handled his business investigations. 'I want protection for her around the clock,' he told the head of the investigative team. The man he was talking to was an expert in surveillance, and Marco was confident that from day one he would know as much about Cassandra as if he were standing next to her.

CHAPTER EIGHT

SHE HAD GIVEN up trying to contact Marco. If they did meet again, it would be on her terms. She may not have his power and money, but she was not going to take this insulting behaviour from a man who apparently refused to believe she was carrying his child.

Being a prospective single mother with no money wasn't easy, but it taught her a lot of things—things she had never imagined learning—things about her mother, for example. If she had one complaint, it was that she felt isolated sometimes in the tiny house she was renting. She realised now that her mother must have felt just the same in the grand mansion where Cass had been born. She only wished she had been old enough to understand her mother's loneliness, and that she could cross time and space now to put things right. Her father would still have slept with all his groupies—she doubted anyone could have changed him—but she hoped she could have helped her mother. No wonder her mother had wandered around in a drug-fuelled stupor. She must have been desperate to work out how to compete for the attention of a man who'd no longer wanted her.

She had learned these lessons from the past and could look after herself, Cass reassured herself, as she closed her hand tightly round the scan of her baby. She would shut her heart to Marco di Fivizzano, if it meant bringing up their child free from guilt and heartache. And if Marco was an example of how the rich and famous lived, she was glad to be poor and no one.

Not so glad to be sick again, though…

Leaning her hand against the wall, she retched on an empty stomach. *Hyperemesis gravidarum*, the doctor had called it, telling her that her morning sickness should ease soon.

Soon couldn't come soon enough for Cass. She was usually so healthy and full of pep, but these days she felt tired from the moment she woke up to when she fell exhausted into bed, and she was feeling particularly nauseous today. She was pale and grey, with an unattractive green tinge, she acknowledged ruefully as she stared at her reflection in the bathroom mirror. Bloodshot eyes didn't do much for her either. She wasn't blooming, as pregnant women were supposed to do, according to the magazines—she felt wretched and too ill to work. Thankfully, she had an understanding manager, but his compassion would only stretch so far, Cass suspected. The upside of her situation was the news from the midwife that her baby was thriving. So she'd keep on keeping on—what else could she do? And she would try to eat healthily—when she could bear to eat at all.

It was all in a good cause, she told herself firmly as she picked up a nourishing snack on her way back to bed in the vainest of hopes that she could keep it down. She took the phone with her to call her manager to ask if she could change shifts, and then she crawled back under the duvet with relief to wait for her twitchy stomach to calm down.

He had called his pilot, who was having the jet made ready before his PA had a chance to ask him if there was anything more she could do for him. His investigators hadn't disappointed him, though their latest report had thrown him. If Cassandra was sick it changed everything. As a past member of his staff, he had a certain responsibility towards her, whether or not the baby was his.

A baby that might be his...

And he missed her. *Dio!* Just admitting those words made him frown. Had he grown soft?

No. He was merely doing what had to be done, and it was a job that couldn't be delegated. After she'd called the office, he wouldn't put anything past her, so he had to see for himself exactly what was going on. The fact that, according to his sources, Cassandra had been living an exemplary life didn't really surprise him, but it was welcome news. He wanted her to look after herself. His experience of women before Cass was hardly reassuring, and it was in his nature to be suspicious and think the worst. When the baby was born there would be a DNA test. He would have to be sure before committing himself further. With a shake of his head he cursed at being the cause of history repeating itself. Because of him another child would come into this world subject to scrutiny, subject to suspicion, and then maybe that child would be discarded...*and by him.*

He stopped outside the modest door and checked the address. Lifting the serviceable knocker, he rapped sharply three times. He waited and knocked again.

The door opened and there she stood. His whole body tensed as she stared at him in amazement. 'Marco?'

Her voice was faint with surprise, but it was the fact that Cassandra was so diminished in both body and spirit that shocked him. He had expected to be greeted by the robust woman who had taken him on and fought back, but this frail-looking girl seemed incapable of doing anything.

She was like a wraith, a mere shadow of her healthy, sun-kissed, capable self. To say he was concerned would be an understatement. 'May I come in?'

Wordlessly, she stood back.

The interior of the small terraced house was as neat as the exterior. It was compact but functional, with a tiny kitchen at the street end of the room. At the other end there was a solid fuel burner with a couple of battered sofas either side of it, and a fireguard already in place.

The fireguard looked new, as if she was planning ahead and buying things bit by bit. A narrow staircase led up to what he suspected would be a maximum of two small bedrooms and a simple bathroom. Her front door opened directly onto the street, and he guessed there was no garden. There was certainly no display outside the front door to say that this was the home of an avid gardener, though he noticed that the pot plants on her windowsill were drooping. Seeing that almost jolted him more than anything else.

Emotion got the better of him, and he launched straight in. 'Why didn't you tell me you were pregnant as soon as you knew?'

'I did—I tried to get in touch with you, but you wouldn't take my calls.'

'You should have come to Rome.'

She laughed. 'That's easy for you to say with a private jet at your disposal.'

'You shouldn't have left Rome in the first place,' he argued. 'But you could have texted me, written to me.'

'How cold do you think I am, Marco? I'm not like you. I had to see you face to face and hear your voice before I could tell you about the baby. I couldn't just type out the news that we were having a child like an invoice and submit it to you.'

He ground his jaw, knowing she was right. 'How are

you getting on?' He could see for himself, but for once he couldn't find the right words to say.

She shrugged.

'You don't look well. You look exhausted.' She'd lost far too much weight.

'I'm pregnant, Marco. Would you like to sit down?' She remained standing stiffly and as far away from him as she could.

'Thank you, but I'll stand. I've been sitting down long enough in the jet coming over, and again in the car that brought me from the airport.'

'I'm sorry if I've interrupted your busy schedule.'

'Stop it,' he warned softly.

'Why are you here, Marco? What do you want?'

'To see you. To see how you are.'

'You won't speak to me on the phone and now you're here?' She shook her head. 'What you do never makes any sense to me. How did you find me?'

'The village you live in isn't exactly a big place.'

'And you had me watched,' she guessed. 'How dare you?'

'You walked out without a word. Is that acceptable behaviour?'

'You paid me off. You only wanted me for sex.'

'I did not,' he said quietly. This wasn't the time to examine his motives, but he had not wanted her just for sex. Cassandra had made him laugh. She had made him relax. She had made him feel young again when he couldn't ever remember feeling young.

'What, then?' she demanded, rallying herself to stand up to him. 'Take that occasion at your charity function in Rome when you barely spoke to me. And then, as soon as everyone left—'

'You leapt on me,' he remembered, finding it hard to suppress a grin as he thought back.

'I did not leap on you.'

'You did,' he argued with a shrug. 'We leapt on each other.'

She tightened her mouth and her face went red, but she didn't deny it.

'Can I get you something to drink?' she asked, avoiding his gaze.

'Why don't I get you a glass of water while you sit down?'

'I should get you a drink,' she insisted. 'Your journey—' She stopped when she saw the expression on his face.

'Sit.'

Reluctantly, she did so. She had no option. She was swaying and looked on the point of collapse. This was so much worse than he had imagined. Turning to the sink, he ran the tap and filled a glass with cold water. 'This isn't a social call, Cassandra. I've come to take you home with me, back to Rome.'

'I beg your pardon?' she demanded.

'You can't stay here.' He glanced around, and by the time his assessing stare had returned to her face it was to see her cheeks flaming with the knowledge that he was right. She wasn't finding this pregnancy easy. She was sick and weak, and he doubted she could work in her current condition. How was she supposed to support herself, let alone a baby? *A baby that might be his child.* If there was even the smallest chance of that he couldn't leave her here— *Dio!* He couldn't leave her here anyway. With her godmother away, Cassandra had no one else but him to turn to.

'Pack a small case,' he said. 'We can buy anything else you need in Rome. We'll leave as soon as you're ready.'

'I haven't agreed to go with you yet,' she pointed out, raising her chin to stare at him with defiance.

'But you will,' he said. 'If you care for your baby at all, you will.'

She followed Marco's glance to her wilting plants and wondered if he could be right. She felt just like them, but it wasn't in her to give up without a fight. She was carrying his child—a child he didn't want—but she had to give her baby every chance. Should she go with Marco for the sake of their child, as he suggested? Was she being selfish, staying here?

'Do you need some help packing your case?'

'No, thank you.' She frowned. She refused to be rushed into this. She had always dreamed of having a family—but a family very different from her own. She supposed now that this perfect dream was yet another example of her naivety. Life wasn't simple, and there was no such thing as an ideal family. The only thing she did know was that she would fight like a lioness for her child. And if living in the lap of luxury in Italy turned out not to be the best thing for her baby, she'd come home.

'Where were you planning to take me?' she asked Marco, blaming pregnancy hormones for the vision of his home in Tuscany swimming in front of her eyes. She even allowed the daydream to progress… That wouldn't be so bad, would it? Tending that beautiful garden as she waited for her baby to arrive? The sunshine would do both of them good—

'To Rome, as I said,' he repeated briskly. Her illusion was instantly shattered as he added, 'That's where the best doctors are, so that's where you'll be going. You'll live in my penthouse, of course. What?' he asked seeing her expression change from frowning to downright refusal. 'Where did you think I would take you?'

'Rome,' she murmured distractedly. He'd said Rome, and she knew that to many people Rome would seem to be a dream destination, but Marco was so different in Rome, and he expected her to act differently too. What sort of life would she lead in Rome? Would he even be there when she had the baby? And how would she occupy herself until the child was born? And what would happen afterwards?

Questions crowded in on her. She was weak. She had been sick for days now, and though her doctor had promised the nausea would pass, she just couldn't face dressing up and living Marco's social life in Rome. But then it came to her that, far from parading her in front of his friends and business associates, he was probably thinking more about hiding her away. He wouldn't want to flout his pregnant mistress in front of everyone. Not when she was his gardener, his part-time holiday staff, a young nobody with whom he'd had an ill-judged fling. His peers in Rome would expect a man like Marco di Fivizzano to settle down with an heiress, a princess or a celebrity at the very least. No. Marco wanted her under his nose so he could keep an eye on her—hide her away from the press, from everyone, so she couldn't talk about her affair. He wanted to imprison her in his penthouse in Rome.

'Cassandra?'

She stared up at him in shock.

'Call me when you want your case carried downstairs.'

'Wait,' she called as he turned away. 'I'm not coming with you. I'd have to give this a lot of thought first.'

He raked his hair with frustration. 'What's there to think about?'

'My life—my child's life.'

'What kind of life are you going to give a child here?' Marco countered.

'What kind of life am I going to have shut away in

your penthouse in Rome? Just because you can't imagine bringing up a child in anything but palatial surroundings, it doesn't make it right.'

Blinded by tears, she turned away. She knew her pregnancy hormones were racing out of control, making everything harder to work out than it should have been. Maybe it would be better to go with him, at least until she had regained her strength.

'Please, *cara*...please, try to be sensible and come with me. I'm not going to imprison you. I'm going to treat you as my guest.'

'Your guest?' As if that didn't hurt. 'Your life is so different from mine.'

'Yes, it is,' Marco conceded, 'but I can't change it—not even for you.'

'You can't go anywhere without the paparazzi following you, and I don't want that.'

'You'll learn to ignore them.'

'Will I? I've got enough to do, learning how to be a mother.'

'It's not like you to avoid a challenge, Cassandra.'

'I've never been pregnant before.'

Her feelings were so strong, so confused. Marco was inviting her into his world, which was everything she had always told herself she must avoid. He was the father of her child, and there wasn't a part of her that didn't yearn for them to take that journey together. How often had she longed for a real home and a real family? But that wasn't what Marco was offering her. He was offering a part-time solution, which would make the inevitable break-up that much harder when it came.

'You need help, Cassandra, and you know it. What's most important to you? Are you thinking of yourself or your baby?'

'The baby, of course. You don't need to ask.'

'Then you don't need to debate any longer. Come with me and your baby will thrive. I promise you that.'

'Give me until tomorrow morning. I'll give you my answer then.'

On this occasion he couldn't refuse a pregnant woman the chance to think things through and so he booked into a local hotel. His frustration was mounting, likewise his impatience with Cassandra, who refused to give ground. He had made several fortunes and had found that process a whole lot easier than this. He had raised himself out of the gutter without half so much soul-searching.

When it came to it he found he couldn't wait until the morning, so he called her up on the phone.

'I've given you my answer, Marco. I need more time.'

'Nonsense. You know what you want. You're not an indecisive woman, so let me hear your decision.'

There was a long silence and then she said, 'All right. I agree I probably do need a rest, but the sickness will pass, and then I want to work for as long as I can until the baby is born. I can't just come to Rome and do nothing. If I agree to come back with you, you have to allow me to choose a job, and you can't interfere with that. I don't want your influence helping me, and I don't want your money supporting me, but I am prepared to accept that my baby needs its mother in better health. So, if your offer's still on, you can pick me up in the morning, but only on those terms.'

She was setting terms for him? He had never, in all his years in business, been in a position where he was on the receiving end of terms.

'This is what I want, Marco. You're right in saying I'm not an indecisive woman, and what I've suggested seems fair to both of us from my perspective. I won't be a drain on you, and you'll have a guest staying for a while who promises not to get under your feet.'

It wasn't his feet he was worried about.

'Are you still there, Marco?'

'I'm riveted.'

She ignored his sarcasm. 'Do you agree to my terms?'

Her place was small but homely, and Cassandra was not a helpless woman. He knew that to have her agree to his suggestion was a measure of how sick she felt.

As for her terms, terms were negotiable. Cassandra's health was not.

CHAPTER NINE

SHE WAS SO sure she had thought things through properly before leaving for Rome, but this was so much worse than she had imagined. Exchanging her tiny, cosy home for Marco's vast, impersonal penthouse was like being stranded on a desert island. The impressive door had barely swung open on the all-too-familiar hallway with its Caligula overtones when Marco turned to go.

He gave her no explanation. Why would he? He'd been working on the flight, and when they'd disembarked he had been on the phone in the limousine. Some important business deal, she'd gathered, judging from his decisive speech and stern expression. They hadn't spoken once during the trip, and were as distant now as if they were once again the billionaire and his part-time gardener.

She cringed with embarrassment when his driver put her shabby suitcase down in the hall before following Marco out. Her case looked like a boil on the pristine marble floor, and when she went to pick it up, a maid as starchy as her uniform whisked it away before Cass had the chance to touch it.

'Your room is ready for you, *signorina*.'

'Thank you.' She felt the hallway was spinning. Everything was happening too fast. She followed the maid to the suite of rooms that would be her home for the next few months.

How had she agreed to this? Cass wondered as she stroked her stomach protectively. She knew that her health had made it necessary, but even so her heart sank as she looked around. She knew how ungrateful she must seem, but she didn't need all this. She would happily swop these gracious surroundings for a few calm words with Marco.

'If you need anything else, *signorina…*'

The maid was hovering by the door.

'I won't, but thank you.' All Cass wanted was to be left alone.

'If you change your mind, please call me on the house phone.'

'Thank you,' she said again, wondering what Marco's staff made of her.

Nothing, she guessed. They probably saw lots of women arrive and leave without ever exchanging a friendly greeting with them.

When the door closed she turned full circle slowly. Everywhere was beautiful and light, and very spacious, but though it was all incredibly impressive, Marco's magnificent penthouse had more of an air of an exclusive hotel than a home. People slept here, and occasionally ate here, but they never left a personal mark. There were no photographs, no trophies, no memorabilia at all. There was absolutely nothing to give a hint of the type of man who lived here. Maybe that was Marco's intention. He had the reputation of being a cold, aloof man.

But not in bed.

That was all over now, she told herself sensibly. She was pregnant. He was suspicious. They were at an impasse. And for now there was nothing to be done about it.

The maid brought her a light supper of delicious salad and freshly baked bread. When the phone had rung earlier she had nearly jumped out of her skin, and had rushed to answer it, only to hear the dispassionate tones of Marco's chef, enquiring what she would like to eat and where she would like to eat it. She had said that she would prefer to remain in her suite. She couldn't face rattling around the opulence of the grand salon on her own, or the even grander dining room.

She had picked at the food and now she pushed it away. Crossing the room, she opened the door. It was all still and quiet on the corridor leading to the kitchen. Guessing the staff must have gone home, she took her tray back, only to find the chef and the maid eating supper there.

'Oh, I'm sorry— I didn't mean—'

They stared at her as she backed her way out again. The kitchen was their preserve, not hers, their hostile stares clearly told her. This was a very different set-up from Marco's country estate, where Maria had always welcomed Cass into the kitchen for a friendly chat.

Marco's kitchen in Rome might have every sort of appliance known to man, but it lacked the one thing Maria's kitchen could boast, which was heart, Cass concluded. If only she could have gone to Tuscany to wait for her baby. It wasn't nearly as formal there, and Maria and Giuseppe had always treated her like a member of their family.

It wouldn't be so easy for Marco to keep an eye on her in Tuscany, Cass suspected.

Hugging herself, she returned to her room. She felt cold and lost. And she was stuck here. Until the sickness lessened she couldn't look for a job.

The vista beyond the floor-to-ceiling windows seemed to echo her feelings. The sky was uniformly grey, and the giant panes of glass were flecked with rain. A stubborn mist had descended over Rome, obscuring the stunning view. Pressing her hands flat against the cold, unyielding surface, she stared out, knowing Marco was out there somewhere...but where? She didn't know who he was with, or even if he'd be home tonight.

And it was none of her business.

With nothing else to do, she ran a bath in a tub big enough for two. The tub took ten minutes to fill, and it took her two minutes to take a bath. Climbing out, she grabbed a towel and headed off to bed. Drawing the covers up to her chin, she stared around what had to be the most luxurious bedroom she had ever spent the night in. It felt like a prison cell.

He spent a couple of nights away from the apartment, knowing Cassandra would be well looked after. His staff were under strict instructions not to let anyone in.

And no one out?

Cassandra needed to rest. He'd been quite firm about that. She'd been overdoing it and she still didn't look well. He had arranged a check-up for her with one of Rome's top doctors, a man known to be discreet. She would remain in the apartment until then. He had sent her a text with the man's contact number should she need to call him, together with his own emergency number, which was manned by his staff twenty-four seven.

Thx. That was her response.

He couldn't blame her for being abrupt. He was hardly a wordsmith himself. The less said the better, he concluded, remembering his mother's drunken confessions once she had accepted that the man he had called *Papa* would never take them back. He had always thought the embarrassing confidences she had shared with an eight-year-old boy had damaged him for life. He had certainly never shared his feelings with anyone since. He would never impose that type of situation on anyone else.

His life had changed overnight at the age of eight. From having two loving, if distant parents he had become the sole carer for his alcoholic mother and estranged from his fathers—both of them—not that there had been any sign of the handyman who'd spawned him once the gravy train had crashed and burned.

He glanced at his phone and was tempted to call Cassandra, but he killed that idea. It was better that he stayed away from her.

And how long was he going to do that?

He smiled as he stretched out naked on the bed. The reaction of his body when he thought about Cassandra said it wouldn't be too long.

She heard the latch slip on the front door at about the same time she heard the maid and chef leave—her prison guards, as she'd come to think of them. In fairness, she had enjoyed the rest. She'd needed it. Once she'd slowed down the sickness had gone, just as the doctor had predicted. She tensed, hearing footsteps approaching. Who else had the key to the door? It had to be Marco. Her heart was thundering. This was the first time she'd seen him since she'd settled into his apartment. Feeling self-conscious, having allowed herself to relax, she quickly finger-combed her hair and bit some colour into her lips, and was then angry with herself for being so obvious. She was supposed to be resting after all.

'Can I come in?'

Why ask when he was already inside the room?

Her heart was hammering so hard she couldn't trust herself to speak. She wanted to be angry with him for giving her no word of when he'd be back—or *if* he'd be back.

But she was hungry for company—Marco's company—and her heart turned over at the sight of him, though he looked more dark and menacing than ever in his immaculately tailored suit.

And more remote, she thought as he stared at her. They really did come from two different worlds.

'It's not too late, is it?' he enquired crisply.

Much too late, she thought, pressing back against the pillows as he walked deeper into the room. He took her breath away. He was so handsome, so swarthy, so compelling, and yet there was danger in those cold, remote eyes. She was determined not to let him see how forcefully he affected her.

'I think I can stay awake long enough to say hello.' She shrugged, as if having a man like Marco walk into her bedroom didn't put her at a huge disadvantage. She was rumpled, and practically naked in bed, while he looked as if he had just stepped from the pages of a society magazine. Catching the pillow close, she hugged it like a shield. 'I wasn't expecting you tonight.'

'I didn't say when I was coming back,' he conceded.

'Did you have a good trip?'

'Yes, dear,' he said dryly, reminding her that where he went and what he did was nothing to do with her.

She held her breath as he prowled closer. There could be no running away or backing off. And that wasn't in her nature. She had come here of her own free will, with the intention of recovering her health. That was why Marco had brought her here… Or was it? she wondered, seeing the look in his eyes. It was a look she knew she should ignore, but her body thought otherwise. And it wasn't just her body calling out to him. It was her soul, her being, her essence doing that too. Because Marco was the father of her child. He was her mate. And she wanted him. She wanted to be in his arms again. She wanted to be lost with him—one with him.

Her world tilted on its axis as he sat down on the bed. He didn't speak. He didn't need to. He just drew her into his arms.

'Tell me if you don't want this and I'll stop,' he whispered huskily.

She might have pressed her hands against his chest in some sort of weak protest, but there was no force behind it because she did not want to push him away. Whether or not it was pregnancy hormones driving her, the way Marco made her feel couldn't be ignored. It wasn't just the sex or the pleasure he gave her, it was being with him—just being with him and being close to him. There was no one on this earth who could make her feel the way he did.

She helped him to shrug off his jacket and watched as he loosened his tie. Breath shot out of her when he yanked her against his body, and she groaned when his hand slipped through the buttons on her pyjama jacket on its way to cupping her breast. His touch was so familiar, and so long missed. She grabbed a noisy breath, wondering if she would ever breathe normally again.

He set about teasing her senses, his thumbnail lightly abrading her puckered nipples. 'Your breasts are bigger,' he commented with approval as he stripped off the rest of his clothes. 'I like that.'

And he was magnificent. Naked and fully erect, Marco di Fivizzano was a big, rugged man, with none of the city sheen people generally associated with him. This was the man who hefted sandbags and hewed logs. This was the father of her child. And she wanted him—no questions, no criticisms, no complaints—she wanted him in the most primal way possible. She wanted to be one with her mate.

She was not expecting him to hunker down at her side,

let alone that he would place the palm of one hand very gently on her belly. Dipping his head, he replaced his hand with a lingering kiss. She held her breath, but by the time he pulled back he was once again the brooding lover. Still, for that one moment he had been someone else—someone caring. Someone she would want to be the father of her child.

Marco soon distracted her. Burying his face in her breasts, he took her wrists in one big fist and pinned them above her head, and then he used his hands and mouth to drive her to distraction, forcing her to arch her hips towards him in an attempt to catch more contact from him.

'Is this what you want?' he demanded softly as he trailed his fingertips over her body.

'Yes,' she confirmed, shivering with excitement, knowing just how long Marco might be prepared to withhold her pleasure if she didn't answer him.

He eased her pyjama bottoms down and tossed them away, by which time she was going crazy for more and nearly screamed the first time he touched her. He knew exactly what to do. There was no teasing now, just gentle pressure in the right place, and a dependable, stroking rhythm. She had no option but to let go.

'That was so good!' she exclaimed, gasping out the words when the starburst of sensation had dimmed enough for her to speak.

'It seems to me that your healthy approach to life and sex is fully restored,' Marco observed dryly.

'Seems it is,' she agreed.

'Better now?'

'Not yet,' she said quickly.

He smiled. 'More?'

'Please…'

As Marco eased one powerful thigh between her legs

she exclaimed softly in anticipation of more pleasure. She felt so abandoned and exposed, and so deliciously excited. She loved the way he liked to watch. It always increased the level of her arousal. She didn't hold back—she couldn't. She had no reason to, and was still exclaiming in the grip of pleasure when Marco moved over her.

'I'll be gentle,' he promised.

He kept his word, and she discovered how extraordinary this new, gentle sex could be. Marco used it to his advantage as he extended her pleasure for the longest time. She heard him laughing softly when, surprised by her inability to hold on, she wailed with shock and bucked vigorously beneath him. She writhed contentedly, beyond caring now—beyond anything but basking in sensation.

When she finally quieted, he slid slowly into her again and lodging himself deep he rolled his hips so that she lost it again, and then again. Withdrawing with a deliberate lack of haste, he paused, looming over her to stare down. His face was masterful and brooding as he watched her grip his arms and work her body hungrily on his. The last time before she fell asleep was so violent she might as well have been unconscious afterwards, and she only woke when Marco swung off the bed.

'Where are you going?' She reached out a hand to bring him back. She was sated for now, but it was lonely in the big bed without him.

'You need to sleep.' Dipping down to kiss her cheek, he added, 'I do too. I have a lot on tomorrow. But don't worry,' he added dryly, 'I'll be back in the morning to see if you need anything more before I leave.' His sexy mouth curved in a smile as he strolled naked out of the room.

He was so beautiful, and so totally un-self-conscious—and yet so quick to close himself off. Tonight had been wonderful for her, because her emotions had been fully engaged, but what about Marco? Was she just offering him sex on tap?

She suddenly felt shaky and vulnerable, wondering if she had just unwittingly volunteered for the position of Marco di Fivizzano's short-term mistress. What else would his part-time gardener be qualified to do in this billionaire's fast-moving world?

The more she thought about it, the more it seemed that her body's needs had ruled her head. She was living in Marco's apartment of her own free will. She was under his protection. She only had the reverence with which he had kissed her swollen belly to hang on to, but even that had started to worry her. A man like Marco di Fivizzano needed an heir. Was she just his convenient womb?

CHAPTER TEN

THE NEXT MORNING Marco left early, as he'd said he would, and he didn't stop by her room as he had promised.

And why did she want him to? Wasn't it better to try to keep him at a distance as he was keeping her? She didn't know any more…

Pregnancy had turned her brain to mush, Cass concluded. She had never been reliant on anyone but her godmother when she was very young—and had certainly never hung around to see if a man wanted sex before she got out of bed. If she had lost her self-respect to this extent, it was time to turn herself back into someone with a pre-pregnancy brain.

In the short time that she'd been living in Marco's penthouse she had become far too complacent. She'd be cleaning his shoes and running his bath next. She didn't even have morning sickness to use as an excuse any more—so what was she doing letting the days drift by?

Things had to change.

She carried her tray back to the kitchen. Who cared what the unfriendly maid and chef thought of her doing things for herself? She had strong arms and a pair of perfectly capable hands, and she didn't need people to run after her. She thanked the chef for breakfast, and apologised for not finishing it, with the excuse that she had eaten too much at supper the night before.

'But it was delicious,' she said, thanking him.

'Do you need anything else, *signorina*?' the maid asked her.

'Nothing. Thank you.'

She closed the door and then cursed her acute hearing.

'Is there something wrong with my food?' the chef complained.

'She's pregnant,' the maid whispered. 'That's why she can't face food.'

'He's made one pregnant?'

Cass froze, then tensed as they both started to laugh.

'About time too,' the chef declared, forgetting Cass might overhear him, or perhaps not caring if she did. 'A man like that needs an heir.'

Hearing her own thoughts echoed sent a chill down Cass's spine. She stilled as the maid hummed in disapproval.

'I don't know why he picked this one when there are plenty of society women who would oblige him with an heir.'

There was a silence, and then the maid added, 'News like this is worth money.'

Cass had heard enough. It wasn't her business to berate Marco's staff, so she bit her tongue and walked away. She had to believe the chef and the maid would remain loyal to their employer and keep what they knew to themselves. Loyalty in any household was an unspoken rule, surely?

The news about his staff's disloyalty broke while he was in a meeting. His PA texted him so he couldn't be caught out by the reports already appearing online. He remained outwardly impassive, but inwardly he was furious. He was a private man, and he didn't care for his private life to be on anyone's lips. He hadn't wanted that for Cassandra, which was why he'd kept her presence in his penthouse quiet. He had wanted her to have these last few months of pregnancy calmly, and in private. No one should be talking about her, let alone his trusted staff—

Trusted staff?

'My PA selects a short list of potential staff members, and you are supposed to vet them,' he railed at his team of investigators. 'You're supposed to be the best. That's why you get my work. You're fired.' He cut the line when they launched into an excuse that the chef and the maid at the penthouse had been thoroughly checked out but there was no accounting for human nature.

Everyone has a price, he conceded angrily, showing nothing of his mounting fury as he cancelled his next appointment. Why was business so straightforward, and everything to do with Cassandra so complex?

Was he really worried about people talking? Or had he finally been forced to face the fact that life was changing for him? It would never be the same again now there was a child in the equation—a child that was probably his.

Possibly his, he amended.

Now he had to wonder why he could never trust his feelings. Why couldn't he believe Cassandra? Would the past always haunt him?

The staff at the penthouse had been fired by the time he got there, but there was no sign of Cassandra. His heart rate soared as he hunted for her. He checked everywhere, knowing it didn't make sense for her to leave him. Where would she go? She had been recovering her health in Rome, and already looked so much better. He called the cab company—he called every cab company in the city—but no one had taken a young, pregnant, English woman to the airport—or anywhere else, for that matter.

So where was she?

Absentmindedly, he turned on the TV to scan the news as he paced the apartment. The news item shocked him—angered him. It focused on him and Cassandra, picking over the history between them. The shot they used of him made him look like a demon out of hell, unshaven and riding a Harley—God knew where they'd found it. The picture of Cassandra showed an angel, fair of face and sweet of temperament—like a martyr he'd pinned to the stake. The press wasn't just milking the story, they were making a production number out of it. He had to find her before the paparazzi swarmed all over her—

Too late!

The news had moved on from stock photographs to live shots. He didn't hang around to switch off the set. Cassandra was in the park across the road, and the paparazzi were already swarming.

She understood now, Cass thought, shoving her hands in the pockets of her maternity jeans as she marched along with her head down, looking neither to the left nor to the right. This must be how her parents had felt *all* the time, not just some of the time. She had never understood the pressures they'd been under before today. She had only tasted fame briefly—or should that be infamy, she mused, chewing her lip.

The papers had been full of the small child playing amongst discarded syringes and empty bottles, and the internet had a long memory, which the bullies at school had taken full advantage of. Even her godmother hadn't been able to shield her from everything. In her turbulent teenage years, when her hormones had been racing, she had thought differently about her parents' notoriety, imagining it must have been glamorous and wonderful to be surrounded by so much attention all the time.

She could see now that those had been the misguided musings of a hormonal only child, looking back at her mixed-up childhood through a veil of resentment. Her parents had thrown their lives away on drugs and alcohol, but they must have been running scared in a doomed attempt to keep up with failing celebrity. And then that stupid fight that ended with them both dead in the swimming pool. It still bemused her to think that it had been over nothing more important than which of them got the last bottle of beer!

But they must have been under incredible pressure if they'd had to contend with this on a daily basis, she reflected as she glanced back over her shoulder at the following pack. She wasn't easily intimidated, but this frightened her. It was relentless, and if the reporters would chase her in her maternity clothes, looking a fright with her hair bundled up in a knot, they'd have no mercy on anyone. They weren't interested in pretty shots—there was no money in them, she supposed. They were like hyenas, feeding on trouble and misery—hyenas with cameras, shoving them in her face. Microphones, mobile phones, television cameras—even members of the public were joining in with anything they could lay their hands on, and all to have a better look at the pregnant mistress of Marco di Fivizzano—to scrutinise her, to examine every blemish and weakness, so they could expose them to the world. Especially her belly. She almost laughed out loud when one man knelt in front of her to get a shot of it, and then darted around to the side to capture another view.

'This is ridiculous!' she exclaimed, only to be hit by a barrage of questions:

'Do you have a statement?'

'Do you know the sex of the baby?'

'Will you live with Marco when it's born?'

And then, like a miracle, he was there at her side—shielding and protecting her, his strength and power, and sheer presence alone enough to scatter the following pack.

'What the hell are you doing?' he demanded, directing his fury at the paparazzi as he tucked her firmly beneath the protection of his arm.

For once she didn't try to resist him as he marched her away. 'What does it look as if I'm doing? I wanted some fresh air.'

'I can understand that, but why didn't you call me?'

'I didn't want to trouble you,' she admitted. 'And I couldn't stay in the penthouse a moment longer with people who were laughing at me.'

'The staff? They've been fired. That was a misjudgement on my part—I should have checked their references myself.'

'And I shouldn't be so pathetic, but this pregnancy is making me emotional all the time.' She turned around, and was glad to see the reporters falling back. She guessed they weren't too keen to take on Marco in his present mood.

'Do you think your staff at the penthouse did this?' she asked.

'Who else do you think would alert the press?' he said as he flashed his security card at the controls on the private entry system. He held the door for her and then let it slam in the hyenas' faces.

'They said there was money to be made,' she remembered.

'A short-term gain,' Marco rapped crisply, standing back as the elevator doors slid open. 'Neither of them will work in this city again. They'll never be trusted after this.'

'So their blood money will prove a double-edged sword?'

'It will,' he confirmed. 'But I'm only interested in you. Are you okay?'

She glanced up at him, and saw only genuine concern in his eyes. 'The staff reinforced my thoughts on you using me for sex—for a child, for an heir.' Marco's frown deepened. 'I had to get out of the penthouse to clear my head—and it did help, though not in the way I expected. It helped me to understand how my parents must have felt when they were chased everywhere by the paparazzi.'

'This is the first time you have spoken about them.'

'Yes. Like you, I suspect, I've pushed the past behind me for so long it isn't easy to speak about it to anyone. But even all these years after their deaths, I feel guilty.'

'You too,' he murmured.

'I was so unforgiving when I was a teenager. All I could see was that my parents had abandoned me when I was small…' She stopped, noticing how tense Marco had become. 'Did I say something to upset you?'

He didn't speak, but a muscle worked in his jaw. She guessed he felt as she did, that years of practised silence couldn't be undone in one night.

'There's something else,' she said as the elevator doors swung open.

'What?' Marco said.

'I can help you.'

'You can help me?' He stared at her incredulously as the elevator headed for the penthouse floor.

'You don't have time to handle everything, which is how you ended up with those people working in your home—'

'And your suggestion is?' he demanded.

Marco wasn't used to people challenging him. Too bad.

She had something to say and he wasn't going to stop her. It was crucial that he could trust people who worked in his home. 'You must try to hire more people like Maria and Giuseppe. If you'll let me, I'll help you find them.'

When Marco shook his head with amusement, she added, 'Just think how much more effective you'd be if you could delegate more. Maybe you wouldn't be so distant—you could make a start with your staff, and then try the same with me.'

She should take the look he gave her as a warning to back off, but instead, she stared straight back at him.

He had to admire her cheek. After her experience in the park he might have expected Cassandra to be shaken and thinking about no one but herself, but she was always thinking about other people—not that he would allow his feelings to run away with him where she was concerned. 'Are we going to stand outside the door all day?'

'You haven't answered my question,' she reminded him. 'Do you want my help with recruiting staff?'

'There's no need. I will be vetting staff personally in future.'

She cocked her head to one side to stare up at him. 'Would I have made it through your selection process?'

Her question silenced him. He stared at her, realising the answer was probably no.

Was that what made him make one small concession?

'It must be boring for you, sitting around the penthouse all day. You needed to rest, but now you're well enough I can see that you need something to do. I'll ring round tomorrow—make some enquiries about part-time work for you.'

She shook her head. 'That's very kind of you Marco, but there's no need.'

'What do you mean?'

'I rang the embassy. To be more accurate, I rang the ambassador's private number. He gave it to me at the party. I thought about what you said, and I realised that I wouldn't be using him, and that I actually had something to offer him—I'd be giving, not taking. I'd be doing a fair day's work, and I would be prepared to work in the embassy gardens for nothing, though he wouldn't hear of that. He said I would make a very welcome addition to the embassy's gardening team.'

'You've got a job?'

'Yes, Marco. I have.'

His protective instinct flared into life. 'After today's experience, you're happy to go to work each day with the paparazzi shadowing your every move?'

'I thought you were going to ring around to try to get me a job?' Before he could answer, she added, 'And it won't be every day. The work at the embassy is part time.'

'If I had found you a job it would have been different.'

'In what way would it be different?' she challenged.

'I would have made sure of the security first.'

'You know as well as I do that the gardens at the embassy have security so tight I couldn't slip a worm in there unnoticed, let alone a pack of hyenas. This is the perfect solution, Marco. No one will get within a mile of me,' she added confidently.

'You might have told me what you had planned.'

'As you always tell me what you've got planned?'

There was a long silence, and then he said tensely, 'That's not the point.'

'Isn't it? I thought we were equal—or is one of us more equal than the other? I don't have to ask your permission before I do something. Or do I? I really appreciate what you've done for me. I know I wasn't well when I came here, and I know I was too stubborn to admit it back in England, but now I'm well enough to go back to work.'

'You will still need to rest.'

'I don't need to rest. I'm fine. I'll be even better when I'm working outside in a garden again.'

She refused to back down. He loved her fire, but it irked the hell out of him.

'What are you doing, Marco?'

Reaching out, he removed the single clip holding up her hair so that it tumbled in unruly waves around her shoulders.

Gathering it up again, she pinned it firmly back in place.

'Am I supposed to take that a sign?' Marco demanded.

'Yes. A sign that I need fresh air,' she said, staring levelly at him until he stood down.

'What about the roof garden?'

'What about the roof garden? You've never mentioned a roof garden to me. Are you telling me there's a garden here?'

'Let me show you.'

He led the way through the door that took them up via some steps to one of the most magnificent views in Rome.

'Oh, my,' she breathed, so taken aback that for a moment she didn't even notice the carefully laid-out garden and just soaked up the view. 'To think I didn't even know this was here.'

'I should have mentioned it to you,' Marco admitted, 'but I so rarely come up here—'

'And you couldn't wait to get away as soon as we arrived,' she suggested, careful to keep her expression neutral.

'Maybe,' he admitted. 'But now you know it's here, couldn't you keep yourself busy up here?'

'Fill my empty hours, do you mean?' She shrugged.

'This is beautiful, Marco, really beautiful, but it's all planned out—down to the last, carefully manicured square inch. There's nothing here for me to do, except admire—which I do. But I need more than this. I need a proper job.'

'Isn't the baby enough for you?'

'My question is this: will I be enough for the baby if I just sit here idle and wait for our child to arrive?'

Marco flinched a little at her mention of *our* child, and then he turned away to lean his hands on the wall as he stared out across Rome.

'You're never going to accept that I could make life easy for you, are you, Cassandra?'

'I don't want easy. I just want a chance to do the job I love.'

He seemed to understand that. Turning, he reached out his hand to capture a stray lock of hair to tuck behind her ear.

'I could admire you if you weren't so damned annoying,' he admitted.

She huffed wryly and relaxed a little. Perhaps they were both guilty of taking themselves too seriously at times.

'I'll try to be worthy of your admiration, and slightly less annoying,' she promised. And then, for the first time, they shared a smile.

They left the beautiful roof garden, and went down to the main part of the penthouse, where she hovered as Marco prowled the room. Tension grew between them, and threatened to engulf her when Marco came to stand in front of her.

'Come to bed with me, Cassandra.'

Breath hitched in her throat as he stared down at her. She knew that smouldering look in his eyes, and her body was desperate to respond to him. This had nothing to do with pregnancy hormones. She wanted Marco, and not just physically but with every yearning, aching part of her soul.

Leaning forward, he brushed her lips with his.

Several seconds passed. It was as if time stood still in those potent, charged moments. Resting her hands on Marco's arms, she allowed him to back her towards his bedroom.

Putting his arm around her shoulders, he shut the door behind them, and then he worked on the buttons of her shirt and let it fall. Cupping her breasts, he dipped his head to suckle through the fine lace of her bra, and then he unhooked it and disposed of that too. Lowering her unflattering maternity jeans carefully over the swell of her belly and her hips, he helped her step out of them. Taking hold of her hand, he led her towards the bed, and pushing the bedclothes out of the way he lowered her gently onto the pillows.

'Turn on your side,' he instructed, 'and wait for me.'

She watched him undress and felt her arousal grow. Marco's back rippled with muscle as he moved. His entire body was a work of brutal masculine art. She could hardly breathe for excitement by the time he joined her on the bed.

Stretching out his length behind her, he rested his hand in the small of her back. She responded immediately, and arching her back she waited in tingling anticipation for his first touch.

Having arranged her to his satisfaction, Marco took hold of her and gently parting her legs he slipped the tip of his erection inside her until he was sure she was relaxed. Then he sank deep. He hardly needed to move at all as her hunger took over. Working with ever-increasing intent, she used him shamelessly.

'Nice?' he enquired softly when, after the longest time, she was quiet again.

'Very nice,' she confirmed groggily, smiling into the pillow.

'Again?'

'Oh, I think so, don't you?'

They made love so many times she lost count, and each time was better than the last. She drifted off to sleep, safe in Marco's arms, and woke to find him making love to her again.

'How do you do that?' she muttered, still half-asleep.

He hushed her and continued to move steadily back and forth.

She remained quiescent and silent, the grateful recipient of pleasure, with no effort required from her at all. She had no argument with that, not when this was turning out to be the most incredible experience of her life. Just the thought of Marco doing what he was doing, and so skilfully, was enough to make her lose control. As sensation claimed her, she cried out his name, and clutching the pillow in a vice-like grip she gave her body over to violent convulsions of pleasure. And when she was quiet, Marco started all over again.

Sex wasn't an end in itself, she knew that as well as anyone. But until a solution could be found to their situation, it was the one thing that brought them as close as this.

CHAPTER ELEVEN

CASS'S WORK AT the embassy gardens was turning out even better than she had hoped. She was smiling when she returned to the penthouse at the thought that she loved everyone she worked with, and was even picking up the language. Working with the plants she loved, with her hands in soil and her head in a better place, she could even start to think of the penthouse as home—at least, for now—and then without dwelling too much on what would happen in the future.

One thing was sure. She loved her baby already, and she would do everything in her power to give her child the best life possible. Two things were sure, Cass amended as she caught sight of her passport in her bag. She had made up her mind to return to England for the birth. She couldn't risk the uncertainty of staying in Italy, if only because Marco seemed to be working harder than ever. He was either trying to avoid getting in too deep, in an emotional sense, or maybe he was trying to exorcise his own demons. Either way, their child would be born soon, and she was determined that her baby's future would be stable, unlike her own as a child.

Marco had been away on business for the past few days, and was due back tonight. The thought thrilled her, even as it made her more determined than ever to pin him down and explain what her plans were. Time was running out on her pregnancy, and he had to face the future. It was a future she hoped they would share with their child, even if Marco and she lived in different countries.

She hadn't been idle while he'd been away. As well as her job at the embassy, she had interviewed new staff for the penthouse. She wanted to earn her keep. She wanted Marco to know that she wasn't waiting for him to do everything.

She also had to tell him that she was well enough to go home, and though she was grateful to him for allowing her to recover here in Rome, her mind was made up to return to England.

Tears pricked the back of her eyes at the thought of leaving him. She was falling in love with him, Cass realised as she brushed her hair.

There were no if, buts or maybes. She had fallen in love, and with a very complex man who was coming home tonight, so she would leave her hair loose…for him.

Marco looked exhausted when he walked through the door. He also looked gloriously striking in a navy suit so dark it was almost as black as his eyes. His crisp white shirt was open at the neck and his stylish silk tie was hanging loose. She didn't need him to tell her that it had been a hard trip. His hair was ruffled, his stubble was thick, and his frown was so deep she knew he'd had a difficult time, though his face lit up at the sight of her.

'*Cara mia*, you look beautiful.'

It was the first time that Marco had called her *his*. Instead of resenting this, she found she liked it, and perhaps more than she should have done, bearing in mind what she had to say to him. She was an independent woman, but she liked the sense of belonging, as well as the feeling that she wasn't alone. The 'beautiful' she'd take with a pinch of salt. She knew she wasn't beautiful. The mirror told her that every day. She was bloated and heavy, and—

She turned her attention back to Marco. 'You look wiped out. Can I get you a drink?'

He smiled and shrugged. 'I should be looking after you, *cara*.'

'Okay, then.' She grinned. 'We can take turns.'

He prowled towards her until she was backed up against the wall.

'Does this bring back memories?' he asked, staring down at her with the faintest of smiles on his dark, brooding face.

'A few,' she admitted. She longed for him to kiss her. She wanted to feel his hard body pressed against hers…

'What about this?' he murmured, scraping her sensitive skin with his stubble as he scorched a trail of almost kisses down her neck.

'A few more memories seem to be returning,' she conceded wryly.

'How about this?'

She closed her eyes and exhaled shakily as Marco's big hands captured her breasts.

'You have the most magnificent breasts, Cassandra.'

'And you haven't closed the front door.'

He put his foot to it. 'Better now?'

As he was cupping her between the legs as he asked the question, her answer could only be a shaky 'Not quite yet…'

She looked up and knew Marco could see the heat in her eyes.

'Is there anything I can do to improve the situation for you?' he asked.

'There might be,' she conceded.

Moving his hands to cup her face, he dipped his head and kissed her…very gently. It was a tender kiss of a type they'd never shared before, and it fired every nerve ending in her body.

'The bedroom?' he suggested with a shrug, pulling back.

'If you think that's best,' she whispered.

'In your condition, banging you against the wall probably isn't advisable,' he pointed out. 'Try not to look quite so disappointed. I promise to make up for it with something you'll like just as much.'

'Are you sure?' she challenged in a whisper.

'I'm certain of it.'

She gasped as he swung her into his arms.

'You'll have to wait while I take a shower,' he said with reluctance as he lowered her down at the side of the bed.

'That long?' she complained.

Marco's eyes were full of wicked promise, and she was breathless with excitement by the time he sauntered back. Drying his thick, wavy black hair on one towel, he had another looped around his waist. His torso was staggering. Bronzed and muscular, she wondered if she would ever get enough of looking at it.

Marco only had to catch her glance to be instantly aroused, and as he prowled towards her all she could think about was pleasure. He knew just what she needed, and his appetite matched hers. Her glance dropped to his mouth. She had never experienced anything like this all-consuming hunger. She was quivering with excitement as he came to stand in front of her. His thick hair was still curling damply and catching on his stubble. She smiled a little to see he hadn't shaved.

Drawing her into his arms, he kissed her neck. And then, putting his arms around her, he moved with her to some silent music. Then he turned her so she had her back to him, and looping his arms around what was left of her waist he whispered into her ear, 'I love this position with your back to me—it's perfect for making love when you're pregnant.'

'Perfect when I'm not pregnant too,' she replied.

She could feel his hard need pressing into her. It only made her hungrier for him than ever. Arching her back, she invited him to take full advantage of her pregnancy-fuelled, wild-for-sex body, and then she rolled her hips against him.

Marco brought her down on the bed beside him. 'I need this,' he groaned, sinking into her.

'Me too,' she gasped out, holding onto him as her breathing quickened.

Marco braced himself on his forearms to keep his weight off her as he stared down. That look in his eyes was enough to break her apart.

'I guessed you needed that too,' he teased her as her violent release shattered her thought processes into a starburst of light.

'More?' he asked as she writhed beneath him.

He turned her on her side the way she liked, and whispered, 'You're going to bend your knees while I sink slowly into you, and I'm going to touch you at the same time.'

His hand had barely found its destination before she greedily claimed her next release.

'I think you like that,' he murmured. Resting his chin on her back, he waited as she dragged in some noisy breaths.

'Definitely,' she confirmed.

'Are you ready for more?'

Marco only had to rest his hand in the small of her back for her to lift her buttocks so he could cup them and slowly take her again. Moving to a steady and dependable beat, he worked her with his hand at the same time, steering her unerringly into her fiercest climax yet.

Cassandra was sleeping so heavily he decided to make her breakfast in bed. She should rest—wasn't he always telling her that? He should tell himself that—he'd kept her up half the night. He couldn't get enough of her. He'd never felt like this before—had never made love to a woman all night and woken her up in the morning by making love to her. Hell, he'd never cooked a woman breakfast before—not since he had tried to coax his mother to eat in the latter stages of her alcoholism, a thought that shattered his current idyll.

The priest who had buried his mother had seen to it that he had a roof over his head and had gone to school with enough food in his belly to keep him going for the day. The orphanage had been a chilling experience, but he'd survived that too. There was nothing in this world he couldn't overcome—with the exception of his feelings for Cassandra.

But he couldn't offer her anything more than this, he mused as he backed his way into the bedroom. He'd been dead inside for far too long to make any form of commitment, and he would never lead Cassandra on.

She woke slowly and smiled with her face still pressed against the pillow as he carried her breakfast tray into the room.

'You made me breakfast!' she exclaimed with pleasure.

Pressing his lips down, he shrugged. 'It's in my best interests to keep your strength up.'

'Stop acting tough, Marco. Even if you're joking, I know you're kinder than you make out. You've got a whole bank of feelings inside you, but you're like a miser afraid to dip into them.'

'Afraid?' he queried, already tensing in preparation for retreating into himself as he put the tray down.

'I know. You're not afraid of anything…except what's inside you,' she said, losing her smile. 'And we all have demons in the past to fight.'

'I don't know what you mean.'

She stared at him for a moment, and then she held out her hand. 'Come here…'

'I have to go to work…'

'Please,' she insisted. 'Give me your hand.'

He frowned, but he did as she asked.

Taking it, she guided it beneath the bedclothes. 'Can you feel him? Your son is saying hello.'

'My—' He recoiled, but she caught hold of his hand, and with more strength than he had guessed she possessed she brought his hand back again and made him rest it on her swollen belly.

'Don't be frightened,' she whispered. 'We're both new at this. Babies don't come with a manual, and I don't want you to miss out on a single thing.'

He'd weakened once before and kissed her belly. He had survived that. The miracle of life was something even he couldn't resist. He calmed his breathing and stilled, and then he felt it…he felt the little pulse of life, trying to kick his hand away.

'*Dio!* I can feel him.' His eyes were full of wonder as he turned to look at her. 'That's your baby!'

Cassandra looked at him steadily for a good few moments and then she said, 'That's our child.'

There was so much she wanted to say to Marco. She wanted to reach out to him in a way that would break through all his issues, but before she could do that he had to trust her…trust her enough to tell her what had made him this way.

'Marco?'

He was heading at speed for the door, and looked stricken. Yet she knew he'd had that same moment of wonder and bliss that she had experienced when she had felt their child kicking her for the first time. What was it about this baby that frightened Marco? What had rocked the foundations of his world? If his only concern was that her baby was his, he could resolve that with a test. She suspected it was something more than that—something so devastating that it had shaped Marco's life. She wanted to know what that was, so she could help him.

These thoughts plagued her, though she went on to have a productive day. She had been allowed to redesign a tiny portion of the embassy garden, and hadn't realised how late it was when she finally finished up. Marco's driver, an elderly man called Paolo, was waiting for her. Paolo was full of courtly charm and he insisted on seeing her to the door of the penthouse. It was while they were travelling up in the elevator that he offered her a small insight into Marco's past.

'He's a good man,' Paolo said, turning to face her. 'I used to work for his father, you know? Bad business, that.'

'His father?' She was instantly alert, but Paolo had already tensed, as if he knew he'd said too much. 'You used to work for Marco's father?' she repeated. She had to try and prompt more out of him.

'Yes,' Paolo offered, saying no more.

'So, how did you come to work for Marco?' she pressed.

Paolo thought about this for a moment, as if he were weighing his loyalty to both men.

'I drove Marco to his father's funeral,' Paolo revealed at last. 'He wanted to show his respect to a man who had never shown him any, especially when Marco was a child and had needed it most. I have worked for Marco ever since.'

'Thank you. Thank you for telling me that.'

Before she could stop herself she had leaned into a hug. Paolo was surprised, but he was Italian so he understood big emotions.

'I'm sorry I can't tell you more,' he added with a shrug. 'I don't think I'm breaking any confidences if I tell you that Marco's father was a difficult man. We were never close, as I am with Marco. But I am a loyal man, and I've already said too much.'

'I understand, and I shouldn't have asked you.' But she was glad she had.

'You should have some rest now,' Paolo advised as the elevator doors slid open on the penthouse floor. 'You must be careful not to overdo things at this stage of pregnancy.'

Paolo saw her safely inside, and when she had closed the door behind her she leaned back against it and cradled her growing bump. There was so much more she wanted to know about Marco, but at least Paolo had helped her to take the first step. She could only hope that one day Marco might trust her enough to tell her the rest.

She decided to stay up until he came home, and try, for Marco's sake, to coax him into telling her more.

CHAPTER TWELVE

HE ARRIVED BACK at the penthouse after midnight, having stayed out deliberately in an attempt to analyse his feelings. Cassandra would be asleep when he got back. He didn't want to talk to her, brain-weary after work, having felt the baby kick back at him. It had shaken him too much for that. Feeling that little life beneath his hands had made it all too real. In a few months' time Cassandra would be a mother, and he…

He couldn't be sure of anything yet. Denied the certainty of parenthood, he was condemned to wait in limbo. And he wasn't sure he wanted to be a father, much less sure that he was equal to the task. He didn't have time for a child. He wasn't programmed to enjoy a traditional family life. What sort of example could he draw on? And what made him think he could do any better than the man who had disowned him, or the blood father who had never wanted to know him in the first place? He wasn't such an egotist that he imagined he'd got everything covered, including parenthood. And he couldn't treat Cassandra as if she were just another business deal to be dealt with and then a line drawn under her. He needed more time.

'Marco?'

'You're still up?'

'I waited up for you.'

She was propped up on the bed, where she had been dozing with her head on a cushion. She looked very young, very pregnant and very vulnerable. He crossed the room and dropped a kiss on her cheek. 'You should have gone to sleep, *carissima*.'

'I couldn't sleep. I had to talk to you.'

'What about?' He frowned and straightened up.

'Your past,' she said frankly. 'I want to understand you, and I can't do that unless you open up.'

Standing up, he put distance between them. All the warmth that had been so briefly between them had evaporated, as far as he was concerned. No one intruded into his past.

'The baby,' she said quietly. 'Our child gives me the right to know more about you.' She paused when he huffed. 'If you'd explain why feelings frighten you—'

He spun around on his heel to pierce her with a stare. 'I have no fear.'

'Believe me Marco, I understand—'

'You understand nothing.'

She remained silent for a moment and then, completely undaunted by his harsh tone, she said, 'Tell me about your father.'

'Which one?' he flashed, incapable of caring if he hurt her now. She had found his wound and had twisted a knife in it.

The expression on his face must have frightened her, as she pressed back on her seat, but he couldn't stop now. 'The man I called father disowned me, along with my mother. He threw us both out on the street when he discovered that I wasn't his child. He did that on Christmas Eve,' he added bitterly.

Cassandra had turned ashen and looked horrified.

He should have known she wouldn't leave it there.

'And your mother?' she pressed. 'What happened to her?'

The look he gave her would have warned anyone else to back off, but not Cassandra.

'You mother, Marco,' she pressed him again.

'She died when I was a boy,' he said quickly, wanting to gloss over it. His mother's death in poverty and squalor was something he preferred not to dwell on. He could never think back without feeling guilty, as if an eight-year-old boy could have somehow saved the situation.

'And you?' Cassandra queried. 'What happened to you when your mother died?'

His lips felt wooden as he thought back. 'I went to live in an orphanage.'

She was silent and then she said, 'What about your real father?'

He laughed bitterly. 'My *real* father? He had no interest in me. When the money tree shrivelled and died, he was gone.'

Cass was shocked into silence. What Marco had told her made her heart ache for a small child who had grown up thinking that he could never hold onto love. But she knew there was more, and even a tiny seed of bitter memory could grow if she didn't root it out.

'Why did the man you called father disown you? Didn't he love you?'

'Who knows?' Marco's keen stare grew unfocused as he stared blindly into the middle distance. 'Maybe he did love me at one time. I thought he did, but once he knew the truth of my parentage he changed towards me. The child went with the mother, he said, and that's all I know. That was how he insisted it must be. Paolo told me that he never forgave himself, that he was a changed man after that, and that it was the shock of my mother's adultery that had unbalanced him that night—that and the way she had tried all those years to pass me off as his child. He regretted what he'd done to the day he died, Paolo said, but he was too proud to go back on his word.'

'Oh, Marco.' There were no words to console him; only love over a long period of time could do that, and now they had to talk about the future, and Marco's child with her.

For the first time she put her hands flat against his chest when he tried to sweep her into his arms. 'No, Marco. We have to talk.'

'Talk?' He frowned. 'What about?'

'About the future, of course.'

'What future, *cara*?'

His words cut her to the heart, but she carried on. 'I can't stay in Rome for ever.'

'For another three months?' Marco shrugged. 'I thought you were happy.'

'I am happy, and I love my job at the embassy, but I have to look forward to when the baby's born.'

Marco's lips pressed down as he shook his head, as if he couldn't understand her concern. 'You've got nothing to worry about,' he said as he shrugged out of his shirt. 'Not tonight, at least,' he insisted when she shifted position fretfully on the bed. 'You're tired. I'm tired—'

'But we can't just let things continue,' she said. Sitting up, she searched his eyes for some flicker of reaction to this, but all she could see was heat.

'Why can't we?' Marco demanded, smiling darkly as he move to drop kisses on her lips. 'Everything's perfect, Cassandra.'

'Perfect?' she said.

'Sleep now,' he soothed. 'I'm going to take a shower and then I'll join you in bed.'

He closed the bathroom door with relief. He didn't want

this conversation about the future until the baby was born and he could be sure he was the father. Talking about the past had brought everything back to him, and he would never subject a child to the experience he'd had. Yes, he had brought Cass to Rome to keep an eye on what might well turn out to be his unborn heir. He would claim the child if it was his, and he would provide for it financially. But emotionally? That was a step too far for him.

He came back after his shower to find Cassandra still propped up on the pillows, still waiting to talk to him. He might have known she wouldn't give up, but while he admired her perseverance, his answer hadn't changed.

'After what you told me tonight, Marco, I know how hard this must be for you.'

'You don't know anything,' he said, tossing his towel on a chair.

He hadn't meant to shout at her, but the past was his alone to deal with. It was a wound he showed no one, and he'd been careless tonight.

He felt guiltier than ever as Cassandra, pregnancy-heavy and clumsy, struggled off the bed. 'No,' she said, shaking her head at him. 'You can't avoid the past, Marco. It's made us both what we are, and you and I have to face up to that. I can't even imagine how terrible it must have been for you to be thrown out by the man you thought was your father. To be rejected like that on top of everything else must have been terrible for you, but if you keep on pushing people away because you're worried they might do the same to you you'll barely live…you'll only exist. You'll never know the pleasure of true friendship, let alone love. We're in this together, Marco, whether you like it or not.' She drew his glance down as she cradled her stomach. 'This is your baby as much as mine, and I have to know what I'm getting into—what the future holds for all three of us. This isn't all about you,' she said angrily, when he shook his head and turned away.

'I never thought it was all about me,' he said as he turned back to face her. 'I just can't see how my past affects you, or any of this—'

'Then you're blind,' she flashed. 'This is a baby, Marco, a precious life, so don't you ever refer to our child again in such a dismissive way. Your past has *everything* to do with the way you're reacting. Your past is the reason you can't trust me—it's the reason you keep backing away from believing that I'm carrying your child. You're horrified by the prospect of a rerun of your own childhood. Even when the child is proved to be yours, you're still going to wonder if you can be any better than the man you called father—the man who deserted you, and your blood father who never cared about you.

'Well, here's some news for you—I don't know what kind of mother I'm going to be. I didn't exactly have the best of starts, but unlike you I'm not running away from my feelings. I'm going to do the best I can for my child—and if that's not up to your high standards, tough! If it's not good enough for my child, I'll up my game—and I won't stop upping my game until I get it right.'

'You don't understand—'

'Oh, yes I do,' she argued firmly. 'I know you care. I know that, however hard you try to hide it, you care for me, and for our baby, and I know you'll do anything you can to protect our child from the type of rejection that you experienced. I know you're a good man—'

'Don't make me out to be some sort of saint, because I'm not. Even if the baby is mine, I don't have the capacity to love a child.'

'The capacity?' she queried incredulously. 'This is the first time I've ever heard of love having limits, or a heart having boundaries. Your heart will expand to include the new baby, and your love will grow.'

Angry and frustrated at a situation he had no control over, he thumped his chest. 'How can I do any of those things when I feel nothing?' Cassandra had asked him for reassurance he was unable to give her.

'I do know this,' she insisted fiercely. 'We can't go on as we are.'

'Why? What's so bad about it?' he demanded. 'You've got a great job that you love, and you live in one of the most beautiful apartments in Rome—'

'My prison cell, with a man who feels nothing?'

Her sad laugh chilled him. He was suddenly conscious of how close he'd come to destroying the vigorous, spirited girl.

'My life here isn't real,' she said in a quiet voice that disturbed him more than Cassandra's anger ever could. 'It's play-acting.'

'It seems real to me.'

'That's because nothing's changed for you, Marco.'

He forced out a short laugh, but Cassandra had distanced herself from emotion and was calmly evaluating things as she saw them. 'Yes, I live here in your fabulous penthouse, and I challenge you with difficult questions you don't want to answer, but we're not close—not really. It takes two people to be close, Marco, and I am more of a convenience for you than anything else. You have sex on tap,' she explained with a small grimace.

'I haven't noticed you complaining. What's your point, Cassandra?'

'That I'm in a holding pattern here until the baby's born.'

'Like every other woman who's expecting a baby,' he pointed out.

'Every other pregnant woman can make plans for when

her baby's born, but I can't,' she explained. 'This isn't real life and I'm not living in a real home. I'm living in someone else's home—your home, your penthouse, which is more like a luxury hotel.' She glanced around. 'You keep nothing personal here. There's no clutter, no mess. What happens when I bring the baby home? Where will you hold your grand receptions then?'

'That should be the least of your worries.'

She wasn't listening. 'Or will I come back here at all?' she said frowning. 'Where *will* I go when I've had the baby?' Her troubled gaze met his. 'What's going to happen, Marco? If I don't take control I'll never know. We haven't even talked about it. You've just blanked out the future, as if it will never come.'

'Stop,' he murmured, drawing her into his arms. 'You're upsetting yourself and the baby…'

'Yes. You're right,' she agreed, moving out of his embrace. 'I should rest—for the baby, not for you.'

Swinging out of bed the next morning, Cass threw back the curtains on another glorious Roman day…the day when she finally came to her senses. However much she wanted to be with Marco, it was time to face the truth: their affair was going nowhere. The light bulb hadn't just gone on in her head, it had dazzled her. There was no more time left to waste on daydreams. She had to make firm plans. If Marco didn't want to be part of them, so be it. If she wanted change, she had to change things. If Marco wouldn't make time to talk to her about the future when they were together at the penthouse, then she would just have to chase him down and make him have that face-to-face talk.

Picking up the phone, she called him at the office. Predictably, he was in a meeting. She left a message, asking for him to call her back, but when she heard nothing in the next hour she firmed up her plans to make her next move.

It wasn't easy to make this decision. She had never pretended to be the bravest person on earth, but Marco had to listen to her.

Dressing discreetly, she called Paolo to ask him for a lift to Marco's office. She wasn't setting out to deliberately embarrass Marco in front of his staff, but as their affair was hardly a secret, her appearance surely wouldn't cause much of a stir.

She lost a little bit of her confidence when the car drew up and she gazed at Marco's gleaming white office building. Her mouth dried when she saw the discreet sign for Fivizzano Industries. It didn't have to be a big sign when Marco's impressive building took up half the block.

CHAPTER THIRTEEN

HE COULDN'T HAVE been more surprised when his secretary told him who was waiting to see him in the outer office. Cursing softly beneath his breath, he wondered what the hell Cassandra thought she was doing. What was so urgent she couldn't have spoken to him at home?

He stood as she entered the room.

Marco looked so menacing, framed against the window with the light behind him.

She refused to be intimidated, though his svelte, blonde secretary had made a point of reminding him that he had another appointment in ten minutes. Was that the usual drill for females who turned up unexpectedly, or was she getting special treatment for being pregnant?

'Cassandra.'

'Marco.'

'Why are you here?'

'May I sit down?'

'Of course.'

Immediately, he was thrown, she noticed, but his good manners came into play. She could only pray they would last.

They didn't.

'What do you want?' he asked sharply, all the veneer of

the gracious Italian lover gone now he was over the shock of seeing her there.

'It's important that I speak to you, Marco.'

'You had to come to the office to speak to me?' he demanded with no warmth in his voice at all. 'We live in the same apartment,' he pointed out in the same cold tone.

'Where you avoid speaking to me every chance you get.'

'I spend more time with you than anyone else.'

Yes. In bed. Her cheeks flamed red as Marco's impassive stare levelled on her face.

'True. But we still haven't talked about the future.'

'That again?'

'Yes, Marco. That again.' She stood to confront him.

This wasn't the young girl he had first met in Tuscany but a lioness defending her cub, he reflected as Cassandra folded slender hands across her stomach. She was so different from any woman he'd ever known that he was thrown for a moment, and when his secretary knocked discreetly on the door to remind him about his 'fictional' next appointment, he was quite curt with her. 'No more interruptions, please. Hold all calls until further notice.'

'Yes, sir.'

His secretary closed the door behind her with exaggerated care—in response to the tension in the room, he guessed.

'Well?' he prompted, fixing his gaze on Cassandra.

'It's time I went home.'

He turned to look out of the window, knowing that if any other woman had said that to him he would be feeling relieved round about now. He felt anything but relieved.

'Why?' he demanded softly.

'Your attitude towards the future tells me that I must plan for the long term,' Cassandra insisted, trying for calm and ending up impassioned—those pregnancy hormones raging again, he suspected. 'And while you seem to think that my living at your apartment as a guest is fine, I want to have a proper home to bring my baby back to—and that means going back to England. This isn't an impulsive decision, or something you can put down to my hormones racing.' He said nothing. 'It's the sensible thing to do. I have to go soon, or I won't be allowed to fly—plus I need to get things ready for the baby while I can still get around.'

'You seem to have it all worked out.' He felt stung, insulted, discarded, superfluous to requirements. He was the one who made decisions. Other people carried them out. Not the other way around.

'I can't just mark time here until the birth,' she insisted, 'or face a blank, uncertain future. I have to get organised.'

He placed a call. 'Signorina Rich is ready to leave, Paolo. Front entrance? Yes. Thank you.'

Replacing the phone in its holder, he met Cassandra's shocked gaze. 'I have only ever wanted what's right for you, Cassandra.'

Cold, unfeeling bastard. She was right to leave. And the sooner the better!

She was in a state of shock as she followed Marco's ice-cool secretary to the bank of elevators. More so when the woman remained at her side until Cass stepped in and the doors slid to. Was she checking that she'd gone? Was she going to report back to her stone-hearted master that the mission had been accomplished, and another woman who hadn't taken the hint soon enough had finally departed?

She was overreacting, Cass accepted as she pressed her back against the cold steel wall. This was what she had wanted. It was what she'd come here to tell him—that she was going home and he couldn't stop her. Stop her? Marco had practically kicked her out!

She was overreacting again, Cass told herself firmly. It was those pregnancy hormones at work again. That was why she was biting back tears. She had expected more of him—she had expected some real emotion, when she should have remembered that Marco di Fivizzano could feel none. She was beginning to wonder if it would be better to cut all ties. Marco was such a frightening contradiction, and she couldn't be certain that he would ever be anything else. He was so tender and loving one moment and so completely detached and unfeeling the next.

The drive back to the penthouse was swift. The traffic was unusually light. She was feeling better, more composed and ready for the next stage in her life, unaware that a second shock was waiting for her. The first thing she noticed when she walked through the door was her battered old suitcase standing in the hallway. Waves of ice lapped over her as she walked up to it and tested the weight. Someone had packed it for her. The maid, she supposed. Marco must have rung from the office. He had wanted her gone before he returned home.

For some reason, her gaze flashed to the hall table, where once he'd left her a cheque. Her heart gripped tight when she saw the message waiting for her. It wasn't in Marco's hand. He must have dictated it to the maid. It was certainly brief and to the point:

'Call me at the office when you're ready to leave. My jet's fuelled up ready to take you home. Marco.'

She leaned back against the wall and slowly slid to the floor. She should have known how easily Marco could detach himself. It was too late to think about all the things she had wanted to say to him—there wouldn't be a chance for that now.

Why had she wasted the opportunity at his office to tell him that she would never shut him out, and that when the baby was born he could visit them at any time? She glanced at the suitcase, knowing that she would still call him when the birth was imminent, and even before that, to reassure him that she had enough money saved to support both herself and her baby until she could get a job. She had wanted to tell him about the wonderful crèche and primary school in her village. More than anything, she had wanted to tell Marco that she loved him. Regardless of what he thought of her, or what he was capable of feeling for her, she had wanted to tell him that.

Resting her face on her knees, she folded her arms over her head, as if that could shut out the world. Deep down, she knew it was too late. Marco had released his cold, empty side, and there would be no going back for him. She should have known that for a man who had achieved so much in life, Marco was hardly likely to allow any situation to stagnate, and that once he understood that she wanted more than he could give her, he had moved remorselessly forward, leaving her behind in his turbulent wake. That didn't stop her loving him, or recollecting every single time he'd been warm, or funny, or sexy, or tender towards her. Love really did have no boundaries, she reflected as she clambered awkwardly to her feet.

She had a shower and found some clean clothes in the case. She called his office, but the same icy secretary took her call and assured her that she would pass a message on.

Cutting the call, she told herself that her leaving was the right decision for both of them. Marco belonged in Rome and she couldn't stay with him, like a brood mare waiting to foal.

But if this were the right decision, why did she feel so empty?

Because there were no certainties in life, and because Marco had consistently refused to discuss the future. Of course she felt empty. She had no idea if she would ever see him again, but she was starting over and that was a good thing. The past had taken a bite out of them both, making it impossible to have a future going forward together. When their baby was born they would come to an agreement, but where their personal relationship was concerned…

There was no personal relationship, except in her head. She had been trying to get Marco to commit to a future he wanted no part of. It wasn't like her to admit defeat, but this time she might have to. She doubted Marco would want any sort of life with her away from the privacy of his penthouse. He was probably glad she was going home. He could get on with his life now. She would call the head of the gardening team she had so much enjoyed being part of at the embassy in Rome on her way to the airport, and she would write to Maria and Giuseppe.

She froze as the front door swung open, but, as she should have known, it wasn't Marco but his driver, Paolo.

'Are you ready?' Paolo asked with his usual warmth as he reached for her case.

'Yes. Thank you.' She took one last look around the echoing penthouse and wondered if she had ever felt so empty in her life, though Marco had done everything she'd asked for. He'd set her free so she could cut all ties with him for good.

He stood and watched the jet take off. He watched it until it had disappeared behind a cloud. He never stood watching people fly away. He had neither the time for it nor the inclination. But flying home was the right thing for Cassandra to do. It was right for both of them.

So why did it feel so wrong?

It was a swipe against his male pride? No woman had ever left him before, but Cassandra had made it quite clear that she wasn't happy living with him in Rome.

Cassandra was different. She was pregnant, maybe with his child. That thought haunted him as he cut a path through the bustling terminal building. She would need consistent health care leading up to the birth, he reasoned, and she was right about getting on with her plans for the future.

Plans from which he was excluded.

Plans that he wanted no part of—not until he was sure. In the meantime, his people would watch her.

Was a second-hand report good enough for him?

It would have to be.

'No comment!' he snarled as the clustering paparazzi hounded him to the door.

Anticipating the fuss he'd create, Paolo had the car waiting for him with the engine running. He jumped in and they roared away. He glanced at the sky in the direction Cassandra's jet had taken. He had never felt so conflicted. When she gave birth a simple DNA test would tell him everything he needed to know. No one, not even Cassandra, could bounce him into making a commitment, and even a positive DNA test didn't point to a future where he committed his emotions to Cass and the baby. Financially, yes. She would have every support. But emotionally…

He wouldn't have long to wait for the answer, and he would be fully occupied in the meantime with his work. His people would inform him if a problem occurred. This was the end of his personal involvement with Cassandra Rich.

He tossed this reasoning back and forth, trying to convince himself that he believed it, until he walked into an empty apartment, and for the first time in his life he experienced loneliness. The penthouse was too big for him. It was empty and impersonal. Why hadn't he noticed this before? He found himself wandering from room to room, searching for something of Cassandra's to hold, to keep… and, yes, to cherish. He should have remembered how meticulous she was. For a healthy, vigorous and very physical woman, she had the organised mind of a scholar. But she was quirky too, he remembered, slanting a smile as he walked to the window to stare up at the sky, and there were moments when she could be adorably messy. Basically, she was down-to-earth and natural. She was also unpredictable, cheeky and confrontational. She was a strong woman. She had wanted to go, and she had left him. She was Cassandra.

He turned full circle slowly in the hope of spotting something she'd left. Had he found a scarf that she'd worn wrapped around her neck, he would have brought it to his face and inhaled deeply in the hope of catching a hint of her scent…

But there was nothing, and he finally gave up. The penthouse unsettled him. It was far too quiet. He turned on his music. He loved music, and this particular piece of low-key jazz usually soothed him, but today it irritated him, because it reminded him of the dance he'd enjoyed with Cassandra. Switching it off, he flopped down on the sofa and reached for that day's untouched newspaper. Leafing through the pages, he barely glanced at them, and was about to toss it aside when he saw a picture that stopped him. A chain of popular low-cost fashion stores had copied the dress Cassandra had worn for the charity event. Just to rub salt in the wound, it appeared under the heading 'Cheap and Cheerful', next to a shot of Cassandra entering the building looking absolutely stunning.

The heading over Cassandra's picture read: 'The Billion-Dollar Babe Version'. There was a snarky piece beneath about the heights that could be achieved by an ambitious woman, who, if she had only known it, could have looked just as good in the chain-store version of the dress without compromising her principles.

Tossing the paper aside, he closed his eyes, and for the first time he was glad that Cassandra had left Rome, so she could escape the vitriol that went with being with him.

He could still remember the shock he'd felt when he had first seen her in that dress. Her transformation had been complete—from no-nonsense girl into a unique and very beautiful woman. From there it had been inevitable that he would remember the sex—the furious sex—the sex she had enjoyed as much as he had. He'd never known anything like it, and doubted she had. It was quite possible that a child had been conceived that night. They had certainly given it their best shot. He had never been so reckless…

With a sound of self-disgust, he sprang up and headed off to bed. Much good that did him. Everything reminded him of Cassandra—his bedroom, the bed, the shower. Was there anywhere in the penthouse they hadn't made love?

Would he ever be rid of her ghost?

Did he want to be?

He didn't sleep. He paced for half the night and dozed fitfully for the rest of the time, and all of it with his mind full of Cassandra. At first light he rang his people to make sure she had arrived safely. They reassured him that she had. He cut the call and looked around, knowing that this was his life now. This was his lonely, bitter life.

CHAPTER FOURTEEN

ONE THING FOLLOWED ANOTHER. It was as if fate was conspiring against him. His workload had never been heavier, and when it became necessary for him to visit the UK to get an overview of some properties he was considering buying, he was conflicted. He had been trying to keep his distance from Cassandra. They didn't have a future together, and it was kinder to them both if he avoided relighting old flames. That she took second billing to his work seemed cold and contrived, even to him, but as things stood, it was the best he could manage.

Cassandra, meanwhile, seemed to be doing very well without him. She was as doggedly independent as always, and to his frustration she made no call on him at all. She was designing gardens, rather than digging them, his people had told him, adding that, in their opinion, there was no reason for concern, as she was taking good care of herself and doing very well. *Without him.*

Each time he sat down at the computer he read these emails again, as if they could somehow bring her closer. Perhaps a relationship at a distance was the best his stony heart could manage, he reflected grimly as he returned to the mountain of work on his desk. While the past had its hold on him, distance from him was the best thing for Cassandra, and though he had no difficulty accepting responsibility if the test proved he was the baby's father, it would almost certainly mean discharging his duty from a distance—which was probably just as well. What did he have to offer a child, apart from his money?

Sitting back, he pushed all thoughts of work away. He received daily reports on Cassandra's progress, and that should be enough for him.

It wasn't nearly enough. He felt as if something precious was in danger of slipping away from him. Was there a chance for change? Or would he relive his father's mistakes, and all because of his pride?

She missed Marco more than words could say. It was as if she had been complete and now she had a vital part of her missing. Marco was damaged and she couldn't help him until he was ready to help himself. She hated to admit it but she was about ready to admit defeat.

Never. Defeat wasn't in her nature. She smiled ruefully and chomped on her lip as she pictured him lounging back in his warm, state-of-the-art office, while she was here, freezing her butt off in a neighbour's overgrown orchard that she was trying to rescue.

Marco could make her life so much easier than this.

Maybe he could—if she was prepared to sell out, which she wasn't. And that was even supposing Marco would want to stick around after their baby was born. She had no idea what he wanted to do. There might be a custody battle once it had been had proved to his satisfaction that he was the father of her child. He should know that there was no one else. He had enough investigators on the case. She'd 'made' his man on her first day back in England. There couldn't be many burly men who would reach for packets of hair dye and scrunchies when caught staring at her in the supermarket.

Leaning back against the tree trunk, she stared up through its contorted branches. Birds wheeled overhead in a hostile, grey sky, which made her think back to the warmth and sunshine in Tuscany. She was as wary of commitment as Marco, and it was going to be a long, lonely Christmas with just the bump—the very active bump—for company. She hoped that she would see Marco again, but it wouldn't be until some time in the New Year when she gave birth.

He scanned the latest report from his people in the UK again. There were no new developments, and nothing for him to worry about, they said. That wasn't good enough for him. Today he felt the need to hear that reassurance from Cassandra's lips. As an ex-member of staff she was still his responsibility.

He called her up, but there was no reply. Was she was ignoring his calls?

Was he going to hang around to find out?

With his pilot on leave for the holidays he flew the jet to London himself. He felt better just being in charge—until he landed and tried to cross the airport concourse, when all hell broke loose. The paparazzi were waiting for him and the one question they all wanted an answer to was whether he would be going straight to the hospital. He scanned his phone. He'd missed *how* many calls? There were seven from Cassandra and three from his staff. He knew what this meant. The one thing he could not control was the birth of this child. Nature would determine the time, not him, and that was a humbling realisation for a man who controlled every aspect of his life without exception.

This wasn't the end of his journey of discovery when it came to the birth of a child but just the start. He was about to learn that giving birth didn't come neatly packaged or with a reliable timetable to suit him. Neither did it come with the automatic 'all areas' pass he was accustomed to being granted. Not one of the nurses in the Christmassy, glitzed-up hospital where, he was reliably informed, Cassandra was about to give birth would tell him when or where this would take place. His best guess was to take the elevator up to the maternity suite and take it from there.

All these practical things he could look at logically, but the feelings inside him could not be neatly organised or even accounted for. He was in turmoil. He was frightened for her. He was so far out of his comfort zone he had no answers, only questions, and producing his passport as proof of identity meant nothing here. He was made to stand back, stand aside, and he began to feel increasingly unsettled as his power was stripped away. He wanted to see Cassandra. He *had* to see her. She was expecting him. How was he supposed to help her if they wouldn't let him see her?

'From what I've seen, Ms Rich is quite capable of helping herself,' a fierce-looking midwife wearing flashing antlers in honour of the holiday season told him when he was his usual assertive self. 'She doesn't need any additional stress now,' she added, planting herself staunchly between him and the labour room door.

'I'm not here to give Cassandra stress,' he insisted, nearly going crazy with the delay as his mind tried to penetrate beyond the firmly closed door to find out what was happening.

The hospital had numerous ways to hold him in check, he now discovered. His passport had to be taken away and verified, and even then he was made to wait until his relationship to Ms Rich could be established with certainty. From the donning of a mask, gown and over-shoes to his entry into a temperature-controlled room where Cassandra was working towards the moment of birth with a stoicism that everyone but him found remarkable, he was out of his comfort zone, tossed headlong into a situation that was completely new—and, he admitted silently, alarming to him. He pushed that aside now he was with Cassandra. His heart gripped tight with all sorts of emotion, concern for her being uppermost amongst them. She looked so young—too young to be going through this—but when she saw him *she* reached out to him.

'Marco…you came.' Her eyes lit up as she held out her hand.

It was that look that stopped him. It held love, trust and gratitude, none of which he deserved, and he couldn't—mustn't—encourage it. Love deeply, and it was always stripped away and denied. Hadn't he learned that by now?

'Marco?'

She sounded concerned, but then a nurse hustled him out of the way. 'You can sit over here,' the nurse told him. 'Or stand, unless you think you might faint.'

He glared at the nurse. Cassandra defused the situation.

'Could he hold my hand?' she asked in that way she had that made everyone warm to her and want to do things for her.

'Would you like to?' one of the nurses asked him dubiously, as if this could be in doubt.

He noticed the glances exchanged by the staff. They knew his press. They didn't think much of him. Why would they when they only had his lurid backstory as depicted by the world's paparazzi to go on? They thought even less of him now a woman of his acquaintance was in labour.

'Of course I'd like to—I must,' he insisted.

He was at Cassandra's side in a stride. Pain he understood. The need for reassurance he understood. He could also comprehend that a new and frightening experience was better shared. It was the look in Cassandra's eyes that baffled him. How could she still feel this way about him when he could give her nothing back?

'What can I do of a practical nature?' he asked the same fierce-looking midwife, now masked and gowned like him. He felt useless, just standing by the bed.

'Be there for her. That's all you have to do. If she asks you to leave, you go. If we ask you to leave, you go faster. Understood?'

He ground his jaw and agreed.

The quiet efficiency of the staff impressed him. An aura of purposeful calm prevailed, and it was not allowed to be disturbed. Cassandra was the centre of everyone's attention, as she should be, and she was everything he might have expected of her. She made barely a sound as she clung to his hand, then his wrist, and finally his arm with a ferocity of which he would not have believed her capable. He was drawn in. She drew him in so that he was part of her experience—a very small part, admittedly, but a necessary one, her unflinching stare told him.

And then a baby cried.

Lustily, he noted with relief.

'Your son,' the midwife said, bypassing him to put the child in Cassandra's arms.

Cassandra had a son.

Her face was spellbound as she stared down at the tiny, wrinkled bundle in her arms.

'Oh, Marco…'

She couldn't bear to rip her enraptured gaze away from her baby's face. She was mapping every feature in the way that only a mother could, he guessed from his scant knowledge of what a mother might do. His brain was still frantically trying to patch together all the new information. The expression on Cassandra's face was new to him.

This situation was new to him. Love, raw and new, confronted him. There was no escaping it. He was consumed by it. He had no response ready, and he doubted that one could be prepared in advance.

'What do you think of him?' Cassandra asked him, her gaze still fixed on her baby.

'He seems healthy,' he observed, trying not to look too closely. 'Sturdy,' he amended as one tiny arm flailed as if the child would like to catch him with a blow.

'Isn't he beautiful?' Cass exclaimed softly. 'I bet you looked exactly like this when you were born, Marco.' Glancing up at him, Cass smiled and her expression warmed him. 'Don't you want to hold him?'

'I'm not sure I should,' he said, suddenly nervous when confronted by such a tiny life.

'Of course you should,' the midwife told him. Taking the infant from Cassandra's arms, she placed him in his.

As his brutish arms closed around the small warm bundle, he sucked in a shocked breath. The tiny child was somehow familiar, as if he were seeing someone he knew well after a really long absence. It was a defining moment, a shock, a wake-up call, and also a dilemma he had never expected to confront. He hadn't expected to feel anything, let alone this detonation of emotion inside his heart. His heart didn't just beat faster, it took off—it swelled, it exploded.

He cried.

'Marco?'

Cassandra's voice was concerned—for him.

Rigid control allowed him to pull himself together and hand the child back.

'Thank you,' he bit out awkwardly. No words could explain.

'He's your son, Marco,' she said, staring again into the tiny face. 'There's no mistaking it, is there?'

'No mistaking it,' the same midwife agreed in his place, beaming fondly as she stared down at the baby.

'We don't know that yet.' He was reeling from reality, from his son—gut instinct told him this tiny, vulnerable child was his son, and that made him fearful. Could he protect the child as he had failed to protect his mother? Could he love his son, as the man he had called father had failed to love him? Overwhelmed by love, he was in danger of being destroyed by the fear of losing it again.

It was as if the air had frozen solid when he spoke. Everyone in the room remained motionless, as if they couldn't compute what he'd said, let alone his reason for saying it now, at what had to be the most inappropriate moment possible. He felt as if time and space had slowed to take full account of his crass remark as everyone turned around to stare at him.

'We can't be sure that he's mine,' he said, reverting to the emotion-free tone he always used in business. He added a shrug for good measure. 'Only science can do that.'

It was as if, having dug the hole, he had to go on digging. The midwife looked as if she'd like to push him into it and then fill it in with cement.

'Oh, Marco,' Cassandra murmured. Handing the baby over to the midwife to put in the cot that had been made ready nearby, she reached out to him as she had done when he'd first entered the room. 'Don't be afraid,' she whispered, so that only he could hear.

He stiffened and stared down at her as if she were a stranger. 'I should go now.'

'Must you?' Her eyes implored him to stay.

'Yes. Yes, I must. I didn't realise how long this would take. I have appointments—'

'Yes, I see,' she said. 'I'm sorry I took so long.'

She was apologising to him? He was deeply ashamed. He had to get out of there or he would ruin her life. He needed time—space—the opportunity to counsel himself, so he could accept the truth—that he was afraid of love, terrified of it—terrified of losing it, terrified of losing Cassandra. He had kept his feelings bottled up since he was a child, and now they were threatening to drown him, just when Cassandra was at her most vulnerable—when she needed him most.

'I'll arrange the DNA test as soon as I can.'

'You'll...' Cassandra's mouth dropped open.

'Haven't you said enough?' the midwife hissed, glancing pointedly at the door.

He hadn't moved. Cassandra had gone white with shock, but then her shock turned to fury and, pulling herself up in the bed, she flung at him in anger, 'Get your court order first! Then you can have your DNA test!'

As a nurse rushed across the room to calm her, the midwife ushered him to the door. 'Get out,' she murmured coldly.

She was right. He was a monster. He'd always known it. He was a monster who didn't deserve to love or be loved.

He stood motionless outside the door, barely aware of the concerned murmurings inside the room. He couldn't be sure whose life he was ruining—maybe all of them. He couldn't bear to overhear Cassandra making excuses for him. But now he'd said this terrible thing he had to get it over and done with. He placed a call and asked the question. The Christmas holidays had produced a backlog in the lab, but for Marco di Fivizzano, anything was possible. And, yes, the answer would be with him within hours.

They would be the longest hours of his life.

Turning up the collar of his jacket, he walked out of

the building, only to find an army of paparazzi waiting for him. He pushed his way through them, hardly knowing where he was going. He wanted to be with Cassandra and the baby, but he knew that he didn't deserve to stay.

'No comment,' he flared when the photographers chased him down the street.

'Is it a boy?'

'Will you make him your heir?'

'Will you marry your gardener?'

'What did you buy her for Christmas, Marco—or have you already given her your best?'

Normally, he would stand and fight, but he had no fight left in him, and to a chorus of cruel laughter he kept on walking. It was just past four in the afternoon and already winter dark. He walked on past his car with no idea of where he was heading. Realising they'd get no response from him, the following pack dropped away. The streets were full of last-minute shoppers carrying unwieldy packages, and while he could slip through the scrum with relative ease, the reporters with all their equipment soon got left behind. He turned his mind to practicalities. That seemed to help. He would have security put in place for Cassandra and the baby. Pulling out his phone, he made the arrangements and walked on. Store windows were ablaze with Christmas cheer, but he felt numb—until a young girl and her boyfriend danced out of a large department store and the boy flung his scarf around the girl's neck.

'Here, take mine,' the boy insisted as they laughed happily into each other's eyes. 'I don't want you getting cold.'

'What about you?' the girl demanded, tightening her hold on the scarf.

The boy brought her close. 'I don't need it. I've got my love to keep me warm.'

He couldn't believe he'd been gripped by such a cheesy

display, and for a moment he couldn't understand why, but then he remembered, and tears stung his eyes as he retraced his steps back to the store. Ducking inside the brilliantly lit warmth, he bought the warmest and most colourful scarf he could find. 'Yes. Gift-wrap it, please.' On the surface it didn't seem much, but the scarf was a vital link to him between the past and what had happened today, and some sane—or maybe it was insane—part of his brain wanted desperately for it to mean something to Cassandra. She was his life.

Cassandra was his only preoccupation as he left the store. He couldn't believe he'd walked out of that hospital ward, leaving Cassandra and her baby in the care of strangers. As he strode along he had to tell himself that she was in good hands. That fierce midwife wouldn't let anyone get past her. But leaving them still wasn't right. Dealing with the enormity of birth and the creation of life had proved him to be emotionally inadequate. Wasn't it time to do something about that? For over twenty years he had pushed the past away, but now he had the scarf and a link to the past that made sense to him. He could only hope that it would make sense to Cassandra.

It was slippery underfoot and bitterly cold. Snow was feathering down, and the wintry conditions reminded him of the night when his eight-year-old self had been thrown out into the street with his mother. He had been freezing cold, and she had stopped to take off her scarf so she could tie it around his neck. So she *had* cared for him. He tightened his hold on the package from the store, and then he remembered staring back at the house where the man who had turned out not to be his father—the man he had loved with all his heart—had turned his back on him without even saying goodbye.

Was that what he'd just done to Cassandra? The thought

appalled him. Far from avoiding the past, he had invited it back and had given it a home in his cold, unfeeling heart.

He stopped walking and found himself on a bridge. Looking down at the oily water, he watched its steady progress to the sea and accepted that life moved on, and he must move with it. Tucking his hands beneath his arms for warmth, he headed back to his car.

No one stayed in hospital for long after the birth of a child unless there were complications, and Cass's experience of birth had been straightforward. Her little boy was healthy, and it seemed no time at all before Cass was in a cab on her way home with a newborn baby in her arms. Her child. Her son. Her Luca. She had given him an Italian name for the father he so closely resembled—particularly when he frowned like this—though in Luca's case it was probably wind rather than general alienation from the world and everything beautiful and gentle and remarkable in that world.

She felt so sorry for Marco—sorry that he wouldn't allow himself to feel anything, not even love for his son. Yet Marco could feel emotion. She'd seen proof of that in the delivery room when he'd cried when he'd held Luca for the first time. But Marco had very quickly retreated behind his barricades, becoming once again a cold, distant man that not even his infant son had the power to reach.

As the cab slowed outside her door, Cass wondered what Marco was doing now. He should be here to enjoy this moment. Taking their son home was such a special time. He must have been even more badly hurt than she knew to rob himself of this opportunity and then to take such trouble to hide his feelings. Even moments after holding his son in his arms, Marco had somehow managed to switch off. She felt so desperately sorry for him. Marco had no idea what he was missing, she thought as she gazed down into Luca's face. Her heart was ready to burst with love. She could only think that Marco had given his heart as a child, only to have it trampled on and destroyed for good. Maybe that was why he had never settled down, Cass reflected as she paid the fare.

'You stay there, love. I'll help you out,' the cabbie insisted. 'You've got someone coming to look after you for the first few days, I hope?'

'Yes, of course,' she said quickly, seeing the cabby's concerned face. He was the type of kind-hearted man who would send his wife round to look after her if she so much as hinted that she could do with some help, and as much as she would have liked the reassurance of an experienced person to back up her scant knowledge of baby care, she was determined to do this on her own. Better to start as she meant to go on, rather than put unfair demands on other people.

But she was apprehensive, Cass accepted as the cabbie opened the front door for her. Thanking him, she said goodnight, knowing that once she stepped over the threshold she was truly on her own with her baby in the little house.

Yes, it was a tiny house, but it was tiny and snug, and she'd be fine here, and so would Luca. She gazed adoringly into his sleeping face, and silently promised her little boy all the love and care that she could give him. But whatever gloss she tried to put on her new life, her footsteps still echoed as she walked into the empty house. However cosy she'd made their tiny nest, they were still alone. She put her apprehension down to baby blues. She'd get over it, Cass told herself firmly as she carefully tucked Luca in to his Moses basket. They'd warned her in the hospital to expect a bit of a comedown. 'It's just the hormones regulating themselves,' the midwife had told her. 'You'll come out of it, and then you'll find that every day is a new adventure for you and your son.'

At the time she had agreed, not wanting to burst the midwife's kindly bubble, but right now alone was alone, and she had a long night ahead of her, with not much of a clue as to what to do.

Put the computer on and get some books out, do some research, prepare bottles, nappies and anything else you think you might need, and do it now, while the baby's sleeping.

She felt better now she'd got a plan. She was bone-weary and longing for her bed, but she had things to do first, and then she had plans for the future to make.

CHAPTER FIFTEEN

'YOU'RE JUST LIKE your papa,' she murmured, leaving Luca sleeping soundly in his Moses basket upstairs as she crept downstairs to make more bottles.

And Luca would probably be every bit as demanding as his father, Cass reflected as she switched on the all the lights to make the place look cheery. She put more logs on the smouldering fire and turned up the heating. It was still dark outside and snow was falling. There were so few hours of daylight in the winter…

She backed into the shadows of the room, seeing a sleek black four-wheeler parked outside beneath a streetlamp. Did Marco have people watching her even now?

She had just turned from the window when a rap on the door made her jump. Crossing the room, she stared through the security peephole and started back.

Marco!

She hesitated. Her initial instinct was not to let him in. She couldn't face a replay of the drama in the hospital. But she loved him. How could she say no when everything inside the house was warm and cosy, and Marco was standing on her doorstep, stamping his feet, with his shoulders hunched against the driving wind and snow?

Her emotions were still in turmoil as she undid the locks and swung the door wide. 'If this is about your DNA test—'

'It isn't,' he assured her.

With the streetlamp behind him and his face wreathed in shadows, Marco looked more intimidating than he ever had. 'How did you know I was home?'

'Inside information.'

'Your people?' She tightened her jaw.

'Your midwife. I finally managed to convince her that I have your best interests at heart.'

'And how did you do that?' she asked suspiciously.

'I talked to her. Something I should maybe have tried with you.'

This admission made her soften a little. 'I don't want any trouble, Marco.' She was still standing in his way. 'My baby's sleeping—'

'I'm not here to give you trouble, Cassandra. What happened in the hospital—'

'Was unforgivable,' she said.

'Yes,' he agreed grimly. 'It was.'

'So, why are you here now?'

'To explain. I don't want to disturb you, but…'

He looked so hopeful, though she was still wary. Marco was the biological father of her child, but his appalling behaviour in the hospital had shocked her out of thinking he might change. It took a large wedge of snow, falling from the roof and landing on his shoulders, to jolt her into action. When he laughed and exclaimed, 'Divine retribution!' she laughed too.

'You'd better come in,' she said. 'But let's get rid of this first.' Standing on tiptoe, she swiped the snow from one shoulder as Marco swept it from the other.

'Ever the practical girl, Cassandra,' he said dryly, turning his dark, compelling stare on her face. The stare she had missed…the stare she had so longed to see again.

She stood back to let him into the house. 'I'm a woman, not a girl, Marco—as I have been since the day we met.'

Cool words that she could congratulate herself for finding, but she shouldn't have touched him, because even that lightest and most innocent of touches had made her long to be in his arms again—to have him kiss her, warm her. At the end of the day it didn't matter what he did or he said, she loved him with all her heart, and she always would.

'Why are you here?' she asked as soon as Marco had closed the door on the cold.

Why was he here? Because he couldn't stay away from her.

'Marco?' Cassandra prompted him. 'Let me take your jacket. Go and make yourself warm by the fire…'

His fist tightened around the envelope he was carrying, the envelope he hadn't shown her yet. It was still unopened. It contained the results of the DNA test.

'Where's the baby?' he asked, glancing around. He was consumed by a ravening hunger to see the child he had so callously discarded in the hospital.

'He's upstairs, sleeping. You can…'

Was she going to invite him to see the baby? He would never know. Her voice had tailed off, as if she had thought better of that suggestion after his despicable behaviour in the labour ward. 'And you, Cassandra? How are you?' She looked 'fine', as Cassandra would say, but was she? And shouldn't she be resting?

'Me?' she queried with surprise. 'I'm very well, thank you.' Her face relaxed. 'It's early days, you know.'

He frowned. 'Don't you have anyone to help you?'

'Do I need anyone? I have friends who have promised to pop round, but I'm still getting used to being a mother and I'm happy with my own company for now.'

'Shouldn't you be resting in bed?'

'I'm not sure how much resting Luca is going to allow me. I will rest when I can.'

'Luca?' he queried.

'That's what I've named my son.'

A steely glint had returned to her eyes, as if she dared him to disagree, either with the name she had chosen or the fact that she had just put her stake in the ground, making it clear that she was a single parent and quite happy to go it alone without him.

'What's that?' she demanded as he stared down at the envelope in his hand.

'I think you know,' he said quietly.

'The test.' She met his gaze steadily, but her eyes had turned cold. 'You had a DNA test carried out on my son without my permission? Of course,' she murmured thoughtfully. 'Anything is possible for Marco di Fivizzano. But that doesn't make it right, Marco. When did you get this done? Did you have someone sneak into the maternity ward to take a sample from my baby?'

'There was nothing underhand about it,' he assured her calmly.

'You had someone prick my baby's heel and take a sample of Luca's blood, and that's not underhand?' Her eyes were like pinpoints of fury on his face.

'I was told that saliva does just as well.'

'Am I supposed to be reassured by the idea of someone sticking a foreign object into my newborn baby's mouth?'

She was on fire and magnificent. If he were in a position to choose a mother for his child, who better than Cassandra?

'Well?' she demanded, taking the tension between them to breaking point. 'Don't you have anything to say about it?'

'I had the midwife you trusted do it. It was all above board. She didn't like doing it, even with a court order, but for the sake of what she called a foregone conclusion she said that it was better she did it than anyone else.' Catching hold of Cassandra, he laced his fingers through her hair to bring her close. 'Forgive me?'

With a disbelieving laugh she pulled away. 'No. I won't forgive you.' She stared at him white-faced. 'Well? Aren't you going to open it?' She glanced at the envelope in his hand.

Slowly and deliberately he ripped it up in front of her and let the pieces drop.

'I don't need to look at it. I trust you, and I know our son,' he said.

As they stared at each other, a multitude of emotions flashed across her face, and then after what seemed to him like an eternity she said, 'Are you going to clear that up?'

Breath rushed out of him as the tension in the room subsided. His shoulders relaxed and his face creased in a grin. He wanted to drag her close, but he dropped to his knees instead and thought himself the luckiest man on earth as he gathered up the unnecessary proof that the child sleeping upstairs was his. He didn't need a piece of paper to tell him what he already knew. He had known the moment the midwife had put the baby in his arms. He just hadn't wanted to admit it—not to himself, not to Cass—and not because he didn't want the child but because he so desperately did. And for the first time in his life he had wondered then, as he wondered now, if he had what it took to be a father—and not just a father but a good father. The best. Though remembering what Cass had said about babies not coming with a manual, he thought he could learn to do this…they could learn together.

* * *

By the time she came downstairs after feeding Luca and putting him back to sleep, Marco had got the fire blazing.

'Sit,' she invited. 'Thanks for stoking the fire.'

'You want to talk,' he guessed.

'Yes, I do.' Sitting down with some space between them, she turned a concerned look on Marco's face. 'I believe childhood forms the foundation of our lives—makes us who we are.'

'Childhood certainly teaches us what we don't want,' he said.

'And what we do,' she countered gently.

'We strive for some things, and do our best to avoid others,' he said with a shrug.

'Is it that simple, Marco? It wasn't that simple for me. I look back and I see my parents differently now I'm older. But my past is well documented, while yours is equally well hidden.'

'And you want to know why?'

'You're the father of my son. It would be strange if I didn't, if only so I can understand you better.'

At one time she might have been surprised to see Marco's eyes darken with emotion, but not now. The birth of their baby had changed him in some deep fundamental way, unlocking some hidden part of him. 'Tell me about your mother. Can you remember her?'

'Of course I can.' He frowned as he thought back. 'As you said, I see things differently now, but as a child I felt burdened by her. Now I can see that she did care for me in her way, but she was weak.'

'You mustn't blame yourself for how you felt about her as a child. You've resolved that as an adult.'

'Have I? I used to blame her for everything—for taking me away from the man I thought was my father, and for not staying with the man who was my father by blood. I later learned that my real father had abandoned her, and the man she married had no interest in a bastard son once he found out the truth about my parentage. I thought my mother was a drunken slut who had slept with another man and who then tried to pass me off as the true son of her marriage. I refused to see that her descent into alcoholic rages and her dependency on drugs was a result of her sickness, and that she needed help, not blame—certainly not blame from her son.'

'And when she died?' Cass prompted gently.

'I was scavenging in bins outside restaurants for our food by that time, and it was a chef who took pity on me. He brought me into the warmth of his kitchen, cleaned me up and taught me how to cook. When I was orphaned he introduced me to the local priest who found me a place in a children's home and made sure I was educated. Education and a safe roof over my head proved to be the key to everything I am today. And in answer to your question, I don't have anything noble to offer by way of an explanation. I hated my mother for what she had done.'

'What happened to change your mind?'

He paused a moment and then he huffed an unsmiling laugh. 'A scarf,' he revealed with an incredulous shrug. 'It was when I was walking away from the hospital after you had given birth that I remembered the weather was very similar to the night my mother and I were thrown out on the street. I remembered shivering, and my mother taking off her scarf to tie it around my neck. So she did care for me…'

'Of course she did.' Reaching out impulsively, Cass put her arms around Marco to draw him close. 'Her life must have been a black pit of misery and she had no one to help her climb out.'

Marco lifted his dark stare to hers. 'It took the birth of a baby for me to remember what my mother did for me that night, and then I remembered all the other little things she'd done before she became too sick to do anything.'

'But you have remembered,' Cass pointed out. 'Learning to love again is a slow, risky business Marco.'

'As you should know,' he murmured, brushing a strand of hair from her eyes. 'I wish you'd rest,' he murmured. 'You'll need all your strength to look after our son.'

Hearing Marco refer to *our* son sounded so good, but she needed more from him before she could be sure that he had put the past behind him. 'And you, Marco? What about you?'

'What about me?'

He would never admit to any weakness, she knew that. 'I've always believed that admitting weakness is a sign of strength. You've helped me to understand you. And you're doing everything you can to help me and our son, which tells me that you *are* reconciled with the past, but you haven't recognised that fact yet.'

'I can't just turn on a switch and make everything right.'

'But you can take one step at a time—as you have already done, and as you are doing, but now I need a commitment from you, going forward, or you will have to leave.'

She paused to give that time to sink in.

'You're throwing me out?' he demanded incredulously.

'To a stranger this might look like the traditional family scene, with all of us snug in our tiny house, but that's all it is, Marco—a scene, and I need more from you than that. We need a plan. Luca needs security, and so do I. And before I make any plan I have to know if we're going forward together or separately as individuals. We've talked about the past, and now we have to talk about the future.'

'What do you want me to say?'

She felt a cold chill of fear, knowing that Marco had always been able to go so far but no further, and she couldn't risk him slipping back into his cold-hearted past now they had Luca to consider. 'You're not the only one risking your heart here. I am too, but more importantly so is our son. And if you're serious about not wanting history to repeat itself, you need to think about your place in Luca's life, because I won't allow you to step in and out of it on a whim.'

She felt desperately sorry for Marco after what he'd told her, but she had a child to think about now. 'Luca's birth has changed you, but I need to be sure of you, Marco. Luca needs to be sure of you.'

'You can't stop me seeing him.'

Marco stood, and he towered over her in a menacing reminder of the power he wielded. 'What's to stop me taking him with me right now?'

'I will,' she said, standing to bar Marco's way to his son.

CHAPTER SIXTEEN

'BE REASONABLE, CASSANDRA. Let me go to my son.'

'No. You can't have it all, Marco,' she said, standing at the foot of the stairs. 'You think everyone wants you for the basest of reasons, even the mother of your son. If you think your worth lies solely in your money and power, then all I can say is that you must have a very low opinion of yourself.'

'You make it all sound so straightforward, Cassandra.'

'Because it *is* straightforward!' she exclaimed with frustration. 'You might be the master of all you survey at Fivizzano Inc., but this is my territory, my home, and I'm still waiting for an answer to my question. What part do you intend to play in Luca's life?'

'A full part if you come back to Rome with me. What?' He frowned. 'I don't understand why you're looking at me like that. You'll be living in the lap of luxury…'

Cass shook her head in desperation. 'If you don't know what's wrong with that statement, I can't help you. Why would I exchange my cosy home here for your sterile penthouse—where I never see you, and where I'm waited on by strangers who won't let me lift a finger, whether I want to or not, and where I'm hounded every time I leave the building by the paparazzi? Is that what you want for your son? Why on earth would either of us want that for

Luca? I may be the first woman in the world to say this to you, Marco, but you've got nothing to offer me that I don't have right here ten times over. When I was a little girl I lived in a mansion not too dissimilar from your home in Tuscany, but it was the unhappiest place I can ever remember living in. I was always hungry, always afraid—'

'That wouldn't happen in Rome,' Marco stated with absolute confidence.

'No,' Cass agreed. 'But I would be exchanging one set of problems for another—isolation instead of hunger, and uncertainty instead of fear. The end result wouldn't be happiness, or even progress—and I'm not just talking about me. I'm thinking about all three of us. I don't want Luca to experience the constant uncertainty that you and I grew up with. Have we learned nothing from that experience? You must have longed for a different life. I know I did. And you have built a successful and very different life for yourself, so why take your son back to the past? Let's move on. Let's take this chance to move forward.'

'That's all I've ever wanted.'

'But on your terms!' Cass exclaimed with exasperation. 'You want everything on your terms.'

'As you do on yours,' he argued.

'I am defensive,' she admitted. 'That's my legacy from the past, but now I have a son to consider, and my main job is to protect Luca. I have to do everything I can for him, and I believe I can do that best here, not in Rome.'

He laughed bitterly.

'Do you expect me to throw up everything and come to live here?'

'No. I'm a realist. I know you can't do that.'

'What, then?' he demanded. 'What's your solution, Cassandra?'

'I don't know,' she admitted, shaking her head.

Something in her dejection touched him. He'd never seen Cassandra in this mood. Had he reduced her to this? Had he stolen away all her certainty and confidence? If he had, he would never forgive himself. It was like taking one of Cassandra's precious plants and crushing the life out of it beneath his heel. 'I will do whatever you want,' he said.

'Anything?' she murmured.

'I won't lose you. I can't,' he said softly and intently.

They were silent for a long time, until he remembered what he'd left in the car. 'I've got something for you.'

'For me?'

He had never bought her anything, he realised. 'For Christmas,' he explained. 'It isn't much.'

Cassandra shook her head with concern. 'But I haven't got anything for you.'

He shook his head and laughed with sheer happiness. 'Are you sure about that? I think you just gave me the most precious gift in the world. The gift of a son?' he prompted. 'That's a gift beyond price. Do you want to see the small thing I got for you?'

'Why don't we check on our son first?'

The expression on Marco's face told Cass everything she needed to know. He was every bit as invested in their future as she was, and though the nuts and bolts for a couple who lived in different countries still had to be ironed out, he was one hundred per cent behind her, and they would find a way to make it work.

It was the first time that they had stood together as a couple, staring down at their infant son. 'You're right,' Marco said. 'He's beautiful.'

Cass smiled with pure happiness as she ruffled their son's soft, fluffy black hair. Luca's face was still wrinkled and pink, with a frowning, puzzled expression, as he grew accustomed to life.

'He looks like my son.' Marco's eyes were steel bright as he smiled at her.

She angled her chin to give him a wry look. 'I suppose if he grows up to look like you, it won't be too bad.'

They left their son sleeping and went downstairs again.

'Do you want me to get your gift?' Marco suggested.

'I'd like that very much.'

'I'll be right back,' he promised.

He felt as if he'd got wings on his heels as he ran out to the car. He delved onto the back seat, and brought out the gift-wrapped package he'd bought for Cassandra. Coming back into the house, he handed it to her.

She opened it and fell silent.

'You see, I do understand,' he said. 'I'm on the same steep learning curve you are, and I don't always get it right.'

'You got it right this time,' she said, caressing the scarf.

'Shall I…?'

'Please,' she said.

He took the length of soft cashmere from its ivory tissue paper and draped the colourful scarf around her neck.

'I love it,' she whispered. 'Thank you.'

'Thank you,' he said, as he dipped his head to brush her lips lightly with his. Cassandra leaned against him, and when he put his arms around her she lifted her face to his.

'I love you,' he said.

'I love you too,' she said, smiling, 'but you don't always make it easy.'

His eyes brightened. 'And you're so easy,' he commented, smiling soft and slow.

'Will you help me to bathe Luca?'

'Of course I will.' Putting his arm around her shoulder, he led her back upstairs.

He only had to take Luca in his arms and lower him

into the lukewarm water, keeping him safe in the crook of his arm, to know that without Luca and Cassandra he was nothing—he had nothing. But could he convince this spirited, vexing, complex woman to join him in a life that would be challenging from day one? Every move she made would be scrutinised and picked over, and every day would present them both with a new mountain to climb.

'You can pass him to me now.' She was holding out a towel.

He did so with the utmost care, and then he caught Cassandra looking at him with a little smile on her face.

'Do I look as soppy as you?' she asked him.

'I don't think you could ever look like me,' he reassured her, as she wrapped their infant son in a soft white towel.

'How do I look?' she asked.

'Fishing for compliments?'

She smiled. 'Why not?'

'You look like a woman in love.'

'How odd.' She pretended surprise. 'I can't imagine why that would be.'

Leaning against the door, he stopped her leaving the room, and bringing both Cassandra and Luca into his arms he murmured, 'If your imagination won't stretch that far, what hope is there for me?'

'None,' she agreed.

'Stay with me, Cass. My life doesn't mean anything without you. I want all three of us to live together, wherever you want to live. It doesn't have to be Rome… Tuscany,' he murmured. 'The countryside is so much better for a child to grow up in.'

'Tuscany,' she echoed softly, her face lighting up.

'I don't know why I didn't think of it before,' he admitted.

'You had other things on your mind?' she suggested.

'Maybe…' His eyes warmed as he smiled down at her.

'Do you think there will be more children?' she asked him thoughtfully.

'Why not? You're good at growing things, aren't you?'

She grinned. 'You're not so bad yourself.'

He was distracted for a moment as he pictured kicking a football about with his son in the beautiful gardens that Cassandra would design and care for on the country estate he'd always loved better than anywhere else on earth.

'Marco?'

'Marry me, Cassandra.'

'Marry you?' she exclaimed with surprise.

'Why not? No one else will do.'

'No one else would put up with you, don't you mean?' she suggested.

He curved a smile back at her and then turned serious. 'I don't want anyone else. I only care about you, and what you want, what you think…'

'What I want?' Cass said softly. 'I want what I've always wanted. You. I love you Marco. I've loved you since we first rolled a rug together.'

'So now we can be a real family and save rug-rolling for any spare moments we might have.'

'I doubt we'll have many.'

'Are you saying yes to my proposal?' Suddenly he wasn't sure of anything, and Cassandra's reply mattered more to him than anything else on earth.

'Luca has to know that love is for ever, and that his parents are for ever, and if you can promise me that…'

'For ever doesn't sound long enough to me.' Grabbing Cassandra close, he kissed her slowly and then with increasing passion until Luca got jealous of his parents' distraction and started to wail.

'Hold that thought,' Cassandra instructed as she headed for the bedroom. 'We have a little man who's hungry.'

'Shall I warm a bottle and bring it up?'

'No, thank you. I'll feed him myself. As soon as you arrived bottles became redundant.'

'So, I do have my uses,' he teased as he followed her upstairs.

'Luca thinks so,' Cass agreed wryly, making space for Marco on the bed.

EPILOGUE

Three years have passed...

'WHAT ARE YOU THINKING?' Marco murmured, looping his arms around Cass's waist.

'Right now? Or a few minutes ago? You have to be more specific,' she teased him, arching a brow as she stared into the face of a man who had only grown more ruggedly good looking in the time she'd known him.

'Right now?' Marco's powerful shoulders eased in a shrug in response to this part of her query. 'I know what you're thinking right now.'

'How?' Cass demanded, though she knew the answer. She just wanted to hear him say it.

'I can feel you softening in my arms.'

'Interesting that I *soften*,' she exclaimed, shivering with desire, 'when the opposite happens to you. You make me so hungry for you. How do you do that?' she groaned, pressing against him.

'Consistent results?' he suggested.

She smiled and rolled her head back, inviting more kisses.

'So, tell me,' Marco coaxed. 'What were you thinking just now to put that dreamy look on your face?'

'I was thinking that this was inevitable,' she admitted, pressing closer.

'You and me?' Marco rocked his body into hers.

'Our family, living here on your Tuscan estate. I don't know why I didn't think of it right away.' She glanced up. 'And Quentin and Paolo visiting on a regular basis. That crazy makeover you insisted I have for the party has certainly produced unexpected results.'

'Quentin and Paolo are good friends?'

'More than that, I think,' she said, smiling.

'Are they with the baby now?'

'My godmother and our two fairy godmothers are with our baby daughter and Luca now.' Cass laughed. 'Last time I looked all five of them were taking a nap before the gardens open at two o'clock.'

'That gives us plenty of time.'

'No, Marco—there's no time! Where are you taking me?' Marco had her firmly by the wrist and was leading her through the rose arbour she had designed in the gardens they had started opening to the public the previous year. 'Marco, I have to look respectable,' she protested when he pulled her down on the grass.

'It won't hurt for my gardener to have a little grass in her hair,' he said, looming over her. 'I just want to tell you how much I love you. And I want to tell you how much my family means to me, and that I owe all this to you.'

'I think you had some part to play in the creation of our family—an equal part, I do believe.'

'If you insist,' he murmured, slanting a grin.

'I do insist.'

'I never pictured myself with any of this—happiness, and a family.'

'And I never imagined I'd find someone like you. When

I was up to my elbows in mud and you arrived in that flashy helicopter, my first thought was to grab my pitchfork and run you through.'

Marco laughed. 'Such a waste of a warm afternoon and a firm, grassy bank,' he murmured, dragging her close. 'But you're right—it is time to get ready to greet our guests…'

She followed his glance to the main gates and the road beyond, where, in the far distance, she could just see a haze of dust heralding the first visitors to the estate. With a cry of alarm she shot up. 'They're here! You've got to stop them—I forgot the time. I'm not properly dressed!'

Marco grinned at her. 'Go,' he said. 'I'll handle the visitors.'

'We make a good team,' she called back as she raced to the house.

'The best,' Marco murmured happily.

With three-year-old Luca sitting on his shoulders and baby Cristina sleeping in the shade at his side, Marco looked on with pride as his beautiful wife, the woman who had given his life meaning, took the local dignitaries and other avid gardeners on a guided tour around the beautiful garden she had created. Her seedlings were fully grown, and had burst into flower right on cue.

He glanced down at their baby daughter, and jiggled the legs of the son they adored. All their seedlings were growing nicely, thanks to the love and care of a woman who was a natural mother, as well as his lover and closest friend. Cass designed gardens for other people now, which gave her an interesting and varied life but allowed her to spend plenty of time with the children. Maria and Giuseppe were more a part of the family than they had ever been, thanks to Cass, as were Quentin and Paolo, and

Cass's godmother, who was home briefly from Australia, where she would return each winter to live with her son. He could safely say that the past and all its demons had finally been laid to rest.

When the visitors had gone she gave the children tea, while he set about the necessary job of splitting logs. Winters could be cold in Tuscany, and he had a family to keep warm.

When the children were in bed, Cass came outside in the burnished light of early evening to find Marco dressed in faded denim, stripped to the waist. She would never get used to seeing him half-naked. He was such a magnificent sight, bronzed and lean, with his muscles rippling. She indulged herself by just standing and watching him for a while, until he looked up and smiled, sensing she was there. He was glistening with sweat and covered in mud, as she had been on the day they'd first met…

Planting his axe, he strode towards her.

They went inside where the house was quiet. The children were sleeping, and a low buzz of conversation was coming from the kitchen where everyone else was happily chewing over the events of the day. They went straight up to their suite of rooms, where Marco headed for the shower. Snatching hold of her wrist, he took a laughing Cass in with him beneath the spray.

'Marco—I'm fully dressed!'

'Not for long, *cara...*'

Cupping her face, Marco kissed her long and slow. 'Do you have any idea how much I love you?'

'Not half as much as I love you. I must do to put up with you—I'm soaked.'

The look in Marco's eyes reduced her in an instant to

a trembling mass of need, and the smile on his firm, sexy mouth effortlessly completed the task.

'My wife,' he whispered against her ear. 'The mother of my children. My friend. My lover. The woman I love more than life itself.'

* * * * *

Also available in the
ONE NIGHT WITH CONSEQUENCES
series this month

A VOW TO SECURE HIS LEGACY by Annie West

And look out for THE SHOCK CASSANO BABY
by Andie Brock in May 2016.

MILLS & BOON®

MODERN™

POWER, PASSION AND IRRESISTIBLE TEMPTATION

A sneak peek at next month's titles...

In stores from 10th March 2016:

- **The Sicilian's Stolen Son** – Lynne Graham
- **The Billionaire's Defiant Acquisition** – Sharon Kendrick
- **Engaged to Her Ravensdale Enemy** – Melanie Milburne
- **Inherited by Ferranti** – Kate Hewitt

In stores from 24th March 2016:

- **Seduced into Her Boss's Service** – Cathy Williams
- **One Night to Wedding Vows** – Kim Lawrence
- **A Diamond Deal with the Greek** – Maya Blake
- **The Secret to Marrying Marchesi** – Amanda Cinelli

Available at WHSmith, Tesco, Asda, Eason, Amazon and Apple

Just can't wait?
Buy our books online a month before they hit the shops!
visit www.millsandboon.co.uk

These books are also available in eBook format!

0316/01

MILLS & BOON®

Helen Bianchin v Regency Collection!

40% off both collections!

Discover our Helen Bianchin v Regency Collection, a blend of sexy and regal romances. Don't miss this great offer - buy one collection to get a free book but buy both collections to receive 40% off! This fabulous 10 book collection features stories from some of our talented writers.

Visit **www.millsandboon.co.uk** to order yours!

0316_MB520

MILLS & BOON®

Let us take you back in time with our Medieval Brides...

The Novice Bride – Carol Townend

The Dumont Bride – Terri Brisbin

The Lord's Forced Bride – Anne Herries

The Warrior's Princess Bride – Meriel Fuller

The Overlord's Bride – Margaret Moore

Templar Knight, Forbidden Bride – Lynna Banning

Order yours at
www.millsandboon.co.uk/medievalbrides

116_MB519

MILLS & BOON®

Why not subscribe?

Never miss a title and save money too!

Here's what's available to you if you join the exclusive **Mills & Boon® Book Club** today:

- *Titles up to a month ahead of the shops*
- *Amazing discounts*
- *Free P&P*
- *Earn Bonus Book points that can be redeemed against other titles and gifts*
- *Choose from monthly or pre-paid plans*

Still want more?

Well, if you join today, we'll even give you ***50% OFF your first parcel!***

So visit **www.millsandboon.co.uk/subs** to be a part of this exclusive Book Club!

SUBS_2015

MILLS & BOON®

Why shop at millsandboon.co.uk?

Each year, thousands of romance readers find their perfect read at millsandboon.co.uk. That's because we're passionate about bringing you the very best romantic fiction. Here are some of the advantages of shopping at www.millsandboon.co.uk:

* **Get new books first**—you'll be able to buy your favourite books one month before they hit the shops
* **Get exclusive discounts**—you'll also be able to buy our specially created monthly collections, with up to 50% off the RRP
* **Find your favourite authors**—latest news, interviews and new releases for all your favourite authors and series on our website, plus ideas for what to try next
* **Join in**—once you've bought your favourite books, don't forget to register with us to rate, review and join in the discussions

Visit **www.millsandboon.co.uk**
for all this and more today!

MILLS_WEB